'OWL'S

OUTSTANDING

DONUTS

ROBIN YARDI

CAROLRHODA BOOKS
MINNEAPOLIS

Carolrhoda Books®
An imprint of Lerner Publishing Group, Inc.
241 First Avenue North
Minneapolis, MN 55401 USA

For reading levels and more information, look up this title at www.lernerbooks.com.

Jacket illustration by Kelsey King.

Design & chapter-opener donuts by Emily Harris.
Main body text set in Bembo Std regular 12.5/17.
Typeface provided by Monotype Typography.

Library of Congress Cataloging-in-Publication Data

Names: Yardi, Robin, author.
Title: Owl's Outstanding Donuts / Robin Yardi.
Description: Minneapolis : Carolrhoda Books, [2019] | Summary: Warned by an owl, ten-year-old Mattie discovers that someone is secretly polluting the land near her aunt's Big Sur donut shop and sets out to stop them.
Identifiers: LCCN 2018038402 (print) | LCCN 2018043387 (ebook) | ISBN 9781541561090 (eb pdf) | ISBN 9781541533059 (th : alk. paper)
Subjects: | CYAC: Bakers and bakeries—Fiction. | Doughnuts—Fiction. | Pollution—Fiction. | Owls—Fiction. | Grief—Fiction. | Orphans—Fiction.
Classification: LCC PZ7.1.Y37 (ebook) | LCC PZ7.1.Y37 Owl 2019 (print) | DDC [Fic]—dc23

LC record available at https://lccn.loc.gov/2018038402

Manufactured in the United States of America
1-44873-35724-4/19/2019

FOR MY SISTERS

THE STRAWBERRY ICED CLASSIC
A SOUR CREAM CAKE DONUT WITH STRAWBERRY-INFUSED PINK ICING & SPRINKLES

Ordinarily, Alfred wouldn't have let anything interrupt his midnight donut break, but something about that late August night was decidedly out of the ordinary.

So Alfred stopped eating.

He licked at the pink icing smeared across his beak and swiveled his head a full 270 degrees, taking in the scene from his favored roost in the scraggly redwood tree.

The sea shushed against the shore below the bluff. *That* was nothing out of the ordinary. The antique sign for Owl's Outstanding Donuts, perched atop a pole next to Highway One, had been dark since 9:59 p.m. *Very ordinary.* Molly Waters, the proprietor of the Big Sur donut shop, was extremely punctual. Alfred had watched her lock up, toss a bag of day-old donuts into the dumpster—his Strawberry Iced Classic among them— and walk the path to the shiny trailer she shared with her niece, all in the usual way. But the large white truck was back, parked across the highway. The same white truck Alfred had seen on two previous nights. And that, Alfred decided, was not ordinary at all.

What on Earth are they doing? Alfred thought, blinking his gold eyes. Two shadowy figures hovered behind the truck's tailgate. Fiddling with something. Knobs? A hose? Human doodads were confusing enough up close, never mind at such a distance.

Then a sudden clank echoed up and down the road, followed by a steady, sloppy gurgling.

The noise was almost certainly coming from the truck . . . or from *near* the truck. And with his delicious strawberry dumpster donut set aside, Alfred could detect an odor. Something unpleasant. Something that should not be dumped into a ditch near a pristine riverbed.

Sloop. Slop. Glop.

Alfred's wings twitched.

The mystery truck's first visit to this particular bend in the road had barely made Alfred blink. During the second visit, Alfred had been too engrossed in *that* evening's donut to pay it any attention. But now Alfred was certain that whatever those shadowy figures were up to, whatever that sloopy goop was, something would need to be done. People can't just dump stinky slop into creeks and get away with it.

Not in Big Sur, anyway.

Abandoning the rest of the pink donut to grow hopelessly stale, he spread his smudged wings and swooped toward the silver Airstream travel trailer tucked among a grove of cypress trees. A row of terra cotta pots containing prickly cactuses dotted the roof, so he didn't relish landing there. But the window box nearest the little girl's bed made for a more opportune landing spot.

She was only nine or ten, and even Alfred was unsure of how much use she'd be, but she was a *very* light sleeper. Which is a useful thing in the right moment. Or in the wrong one.

The pink peony curtains at the girl's window were shut tight, but Alfred knew how to remedy that.

Tap-tap-tap. Alfred rapped his beak against her dusty windowpane.

Mattie was dreaming about her mother. Mom shaking her awake. Mom telling her to finish an endless breakfast. Holding Mattie's hand and hurrying her. They were late, and Mom didn't notice that Mattie was still in pajamas—

Mattie's eyes popped open. She wanted to close them again right away. Even late-for-school-wearing-your-pajamas dreams were good if they had her mom in them. Mattie tucked her nose under her down comforter and tried to fall back asleep.

But something was at her window, tap-tapping her awake and taking Mom away.

Mattie flung her covers aside and crouched by the window, listening with one ear. Nothing. She snapped the pink curtains open and pressed her nose to the black glass.

A face with huge golden eyes was peeping through the petunias in the window box.

Mattie screeched and tumbled backwards. The whole trailer shook as she bumped onto the braided rag-rug below her bed.

The golden eyes kept blinking through the dark window.

Mattie's hazel green eyes blinked back.

The owl—that's what Mattie thought it was— hooted a deep, owly whooo, scraped at the window with a curved talon, and spun its head toward the highway. Once, twice, three times, like a broken toy. And for some reason the feathers around the owl's beak were . . . pink?

Mattie scrambled back to her bed for a closer look, but by then the owl had disappeared. Trampled flowers in the window box were the only sign that the bird had been there at all. Mattie shoved the window open, squinting out into the dark.

Past the ferns outside their trailer and across the empty parking lot sat Owl's Outstanding Donuts. Like everything else on the near side of the highway, Aunt Molly's shop was quiet and closed up. On the far side of the highway, a wall of redwood trees stood dark and still, the start of a forest that stretched for miles.

Nothing weird there.

Who-who-whooo. The owl hooted again. It must have stayed near the trailer, but Mattie still couldn't see it. But from the corner of her bed, up on her knees, she *could* see a light flickering on the opposite side of the highway, the only lamppost before the road twisted off into the trees. And just beyond its glow, a truck had pulled off onto the shoulder. Mattie bit down on her bottom lip.

That's maybe weird, she thought. If they were having car trouble, why didn't they just pull into the parking lot?

A round shadowy someone in a hooded sweatshirt was grappling with the end of what looked like a big floppy hose.

Mattie noticed a taller someone too . . . standing watch?

"Well, that's for sure suspicious," she mumbled.

Then one of Aunt Molly's terra cotta pots flew off the top of the trailer like a cannonball. Mattie watched its little pointy cactus spinning end over end until the pot smashed to bits on the wooden deck outside.

The crash of clay made Mattie flinch, and the shadowy figures down the road heard it too. The taller one shoved the stubby one, looking left, right, and behind. They jogged around to the cab of the truck and dove inside, slamming the doors behind them. Mattie tried to read the license plate as the truck's engine revved, but it was too dark outside and the truck was too far away for Mattie to see any numbers. The truck fishtailed in the gravel, pulled onto the road, and squealed out of sight, with its floppy hose trailing like a tail.

Mattie squished her face against the window's bug screen, trying to peek at the top of the trailer. Did that owl push the flowerpot? she wondered. Her heart kept flip-flopping against her mom's old T-shirt.

Right then, Aunt Molly padded across the trailer floor in her blue bunny pajamas and bare feet, rubbing at her eyes.

"What on Earth," said Aunt Molly, "are you doing out of bed?"

THE BANANA SLUG BAR
A YEASTED DONUT FILLED WITH BANANA CUSTARD AND COVERED WITH COCONUT-FLAVORED YELLOW ICING

Sunday morning light, which is always lazier than Saturday morning light, snuck slantwise through the front window of Owl's Outstanding Donuts. Mattie slumped in the slippery vinyl booth with her feet up on the bench across from her. The sparkly blue Formica tabletop was so bright it made her blink. The shop's sloped display case, filled with rows and rows of Aunt Molly's colorful donuts, was cheery as ever. But Mattie couldn't get the images of a pink-smudged owl, a flying cactus, and a white truck out of her brain.

Aunt Molly plunked a plain cake donut and a glass of chocolate soy milk in front of Mattie. "Tired, kid?"

"No," said Mattie, covering a yawn.

"Mm–hmm," Aunt Molly said, slipping back behind the counter. "Tell me about that dream."

Mattie didn't bother to say that she was sure—well, almost sure—that it was no-way a dream. They'd cleaned up the broken clay pot together early that morning, so she *knew* that part was real. Aunt Molly had rescued the battered cactus, plopped it into a new pot, and lined it up on top of the trailer with the others. She said maybe a raccoon had knocked it down. But Mattie knew the sound of a raccoon bumping around on top of the trailer.

That was no raccoon.

"Well, first there was this owl," Mattie said. "I think it had been eating one of your strawberry donuts or something, and it knocked on the window by my bed and woke me up, and then there was this weird truck, and I bet the owl *wanted* me to see it, because . . ."

Aunt Molly laughed and ducked down to fill a shelf with her Sunday special: Slug Bars. Her voice floated up over the edge of the counter. "The owl was eating a donut, but the *truck* was weird?"

Mattie took a bite of her perfect plain donut, swallowed, and had a sip of chocolate milk. "That's why the owl was pointing it out," she said before taking another bite. "I think that truck was up to something. Why would it be pulled off the road, anyway? It didn't have a flat tire. It went zooming away when that pot broke. We should call the county sheriff."

Aunt Molly shook her head. "Kiddo, we're not getting the sheriff's department all the way down here over a dream."

Mattie's cheeks got hot, and she kept her eyes on the donut in front of her. After her mom's accident, she may have called the county sheriff's office a little too much, asking for updates on the hit-and-run investigation. Aunt Molly hadn't exactly told Mattie she was being a pest—Molly wanted to know what happened too—but after a while she did tell Mattie it had to stop. All the calling.

So Mattie didn't push the idea of calling the sheriff's department any more that morning. Aunt Molly seemed relieved. Then she smiled a little crooked smile. "Your mom used to have funny dreams about animals too, but they never had her hopping out of bed in the middle of the night."

Aunt Molly stopped lining up the bars, which looked just like the gooey banana slugs that came creeping through Big Sur every spring.

Mattie squirmed a little, hearing Aunt Molly mention Mom. Most days, she and Aunt Molly only talked about her at home, just before bed. It was easier that way. So Mattie tried to make what she had seen into a joke, when what she really wanted was to be taken seriously. "No, I swear by all that is holey and sweet. It's not a story. That hooty owl woke me up, and its beak was all pink with icing, and it looked down the road at the white truck . . ."

The string of copper bells on the front door tinkled, and a young couple came in, followed by a whole rush of morning customers. Martín, who helped run the shop most days, was in back frying up a new batch of donuts, so Aunt Molly gave Mattie an I'll-see-about-you-later look and greeted her visitors. Mattie let her shoulders slump and snuck a look at the couple at the front of the line. She had them pegged as tourists even before they ordered the Banana Slug Bars.

Mattie could tell a lot about people who came into Owl's just from their choice of donut and drink. Tourists were their own category. When you were home, you might be a simple, classic cake donut, but on vacation you could be a silly Slug Bar. Mattie and her mom had *always* ordered Slug Bars when they drove from Monterey to visit Aunt Molly in the summers. Slug Bars and swimming in the river and giggly sleepovers with Mom and Aunt Molly felt like forever ago. The thought of those trips was stranger to Mattie now than an owl with icing on its feathers.

She'd rather pay attention to the line of customers.

After Aunt Molly sold a Strawberry Iced Classic and a plain milk to a cute little boy with his parents (who got matching maple bars and coffee, which put them in the happy and relaxed category), one of the shop's most interesting customers came in. Mattie called him Mr. Slug, because he always wore a yellow checked shirt like he was going to church or something. He had a big belly and a ring of hair like powdered sugar around his bald head. He came in every month or so, pestering Aunt Molly about her recipe for Banana Slug Bars. Had she changed it since taking over from the old owner? What kind of flour did she use now?

He always bought four Slug Bars, and Aunt Molly always smirk-smiled at him and teased that maybe *next time* she'd share her recipe. But she never gave up the goods. Mattie knew for a fact that Molly had changed the recipe, just a little, when she took over the shop three years ago. Grandma Lillian and Grandpa Herman had started Owl's together a *long* time before that. Almost everything had stayed the same as it was when Mattie was very little, but the new and improved Slug Bars were so good that even Grandma Lillian would have agreed with the change. Still, sometimes Aunt Molly made them the old way, Grandma's way, when Mattie wanted.

Aunt Molly said that Mr. Slug was a retired baker. He'd even told her that he'd been a friend of Grandma's. Still, no way was Molly sharing the recipe. Mattie figured that Mr. Slug must have had a crush on Grandma Lillian and missed her old Slug Bars. It was sweet and a little sad. Something she could understand.

Next came Mrs. Mantooth, who had bought the land south of the donut shop two years ago and put in the weirdest and fanciest house Mattie had ever seen. It was half built into the steep hillside, like a cave. Aunt Molly said that Mrs. Mantooth had a swimming pool inside too. She always dressed like she was living in a yoga magazine, but her hands were splotchy with old-person freckles.

Mattie knew without listening that Mrs. Mantooth would order a glass of ice water *with* lemon and a single donut hole *without* sprinkles. Since she was a neighbor—and nobody in the history of time had ever ordered just a single donut hole—Aunt Molly never charged Mrs. Mantooth. That woman wasn't there for the food anyway. She was there to complain about one of the two things her property shared with the donut shop.

The well or the driveway.

That morning, Mrs. Mantooth was complaining about the well. She said she thought it needed a new pump, because the one they had was making a rattling noise. The pump stood on the ground between the donut shop and the riverbank like a friendly robot. It whooshed and clanked as it sucked up water for the well from underneath the river, but Mattie wouldn't say that it rattled. She took another bite of her plain donut and smirked as Aunt Molly gave Mrs. Mantooth exactly one donut hole for zero dollars.

No way could they afford a new pump. Mattie didn't think they needed one either. If Mrs. Mantooth wanted to fill her fancy pool and take a shower at the same time, then she'd have to buy that pump herself—which was something Mattie didn't think she'd really ever do, because who orders a single donut hole?

A cheapskate. Big fancy house or not.

Mrs. Mantooth swooped out in a huff, leaving her ice water on the counter. Mattie watched through the window as she folded the top of the donut bag down over and over before throwing it into the trash.

She didn't even eat her donut. Jeez.

While Mattie watched Mrs. Mantooth march toward her driveway, a big motor home swayed around the bend in the highway. Its wide black tires sent some gravel flying just where that mysterious truck had been parked the night before. Mattie hopped up onto her knees and leaned against the window to get a better view. There was nothing special about that part of the road so far as she could tell. Not at all. Which made the truck from last night seem even more suspicious.

The morning-rush customers jingled out the door.

Aunt Molly wiped down the counter.

"If we can't call the sheriff, could we call somebody else?" Mattie said. "Like the mayor or something? You wouldn't need to say anything about the owl part if you don't think they'd believe it. It's that truck I'm worried about."

Aunt Molly scrunched her mouth into a worried squiggle, and Mattie was immediately sorry she'd said anything. She slumped a little lower in her booth.

"Mattie," Molly said, "This dream about the owl—"

"It wasn't a—" Mattie started.

"Was your owl dream last night really a funny one?" Aunt Molly continued. "Or was it scary? Is that what's got you so worried?"

Mattie didn't know how to answer. Lately, admitting to being worried meant talking about things she didn't really know how to talk about. She froze like a deer peeking through the redwoods. Like Aunt Molly might not say anything else if Mattie stopped blinking.

But her stillness only made Aunt Molly say, "Mattie, if that other dream is back, you don't have to start school in two weeks. You don't have to take the bus if you're not ready."

"But, you said!" Mattie shot up, squeaking against the vinyl seat. "Sasha and Beanie are expecting me to go with them. It wasn't a nightmare last night—I swear . . ."

"Okay, okay." Aunt Molly held up her hands. "I just think you shouldn't rush it. Sasha and Beatrice would understand."

Mattie vowed silently to keep any more midnight owl sightings to herself. She didn't want to give Aunt Molly a reason to think that the nightmare, the one she'd had the first few months after Mom died, was back. And it really was gone. July and August had been one-hundred-percent nightmare-free. But she could see how Aunt Molly would get confused.

Mattie's dream had always been the same. She was in the back of her mom's old car and she thought Mom was driving it, but then all the doors flew open.

And Mom was gone.

The car kept running, and the highway slid past in a blur. Every curve of the road filled Mattie with a horrible swoop, like she was falling. She had to stop the car. She had to get out. Mattie yanked at her seatbelt, but it was stuck. The car sped up and swerved. There was a crunch.

And Mattie woke up shivery with sweat.

Anyway, that dream was gone. Mattie had still avoided cars and trucks and buses all summer, it was true. When the dream started, she had been nervous about riding in them. But she'd decided that wasn't going to stop her from taking the school bus up Highway One. She was going to Pacific Valley Elementary, period.

There were exactly eight days of summer left, not two weeks like Aunt Molly had said. That still gave Mattie enough time to get ready. Beanie, who wasn't even seven, might understand if Mattie chickened out about riding the school bus. But Sasha was almost eleven. Sasha was Mattie's best friend in Big Sur, and no way would she be happy if Mattie didn't start fifth grade with her.

When Mattie had lived in Monterey, she had wished she could go to school in Big Sur with Sasha and Beanie, her summer friends. But now part of her wondered if it was okay to be happy about something even though her mom was gone. Maybe she wasn't supposed to want anything. Not donuts, not friends, not new pencils and a new school.

But she wanted to start school anyway, even if it made her feel guilty somehow. Even if it meant riding a bus on the highway. So she decided not to think or dream or talk about anything owl-related. Especially not with Aunt Molly. She wouldn't say anything that could make people think she was still scared.

"Can I go to Sasha and Beanie's?" Mattie asked. "It's Sunday, and Sasha said I could help check in the new campers, and Mrs. Little is going to pay us and everything."

Aunt Molly sighed. "Yes. Fine." She bent down and slid two matching donuts into a bag. "Take these."

Mattie hopped up, grabbed the white paper bag with a crunchy crumple, and swung through the door before Aunt Molly could change her mind.

THE CHOCOLATE RAINBOW
A FIRM CAKE DONUT WITH COCOA ICING AND A RAINBOW OF FIESTA SPRINKLES. CLASSIC, SIMPLE, AND FUN!

Outside, Mattie smirked. Mrs. Mantooth was still at the edge of the parking lot, wiping off her driveway's oversized *No Trespassing* sign. Before she had even built her fancy house, she'd posted the sign right where Aunt Molly's asphalt became her dusty gravel. Mattie didn't know why she bothered. Most customers still backed the butts of their cars into her driveway, just a *little* bit, before turning out onto the road.

Mrs. Mantooth complained constantly that visitors to the donut shop were damaging her road. Her rocks. But even if they were, how would that be Aunt Molly's fault?

Mattie gave the parking lot one last look before turning toward Sasha and Beanie's place. She laughed a little, seeing a shiny red car slip into the lot.

It was the real estate agent, Adelaide Sharpe.

This really was not Aunt Molly's day.

No matter how many times Ms. Sharpe visited in her

shiny high-heeled shoes, Aunt Molly could not convince her that they would never sell the little slip of land along the highway. Adelaide Sharpe was not someone who knew how to give up.

Anyway, Mattie wasn't sorry to miss *that lady's* visit to Owl's, so she hurried across the parking lot.

She didn't have to take a bus or ride in a car to get to Sasha and Beanie's place. She didn't even need to walk along the highway, with all those cars and trucks and motor homes careening past—which was a good thing, because she wouldn't have. All Mattie had to do was hurry past Aunt Molly's shiny trailer, swoop along the dirt path to the riverbank, and hop down the steep stone steps to the Big Sur riverbed. Halfway through August, the water was shallow and lazy but still as cold and black as the back of an old mirror.

Mattie slipped off her shoes and left them on the last stone step before the river.

Holding the white paper bag of donuts above the splashing water, Mattie made her way downstream toward the Little Family Campground. With every soft sploink of her bare feet in the water, she thought about that odd owl and the mysterious truck. She couldn't help it. Mattie could still hear the tapping on her window, the smash of the pot, and the squeal of the truck swinging around the bend.

It had to be real.

Maybe she should try telling Sasha and Beanie.

But what would they say?

Beanie would believe anything. Her birthday was coming up in a few days, and Sasha had her convinced that she was about to turn ten. That she'd finally reach double digits. Mattie didn't have the heart to tell Beanie she was only going to be seven. Calendars weren't something Beanie really *got* yet. Anyway, convincing Beanie wasn't going to be a problem. Mattie was not so sure about Sasha. So she'd better not to say anything. What if word got back to Aunt Molly? Beanie wouldn't *tell*, not on purpose, but no way did she know how to keep quiet.

Well, Mattie did.

Mattie passed the battered white sign for the Little Family Campground posted at the base of a redwood tree on the nearest bank. Next, she walked under the netted bridge that swung over the river like a giant drooping hammock. Green plastic chairs littered the low banks. Here and there, chairs stood in the shallow river too, dragged there by campers, mostly old ladies in flowery swimsuits with skirts attached.

Mattie made her way across the river, toward the campground side. In the middle, the cold water was still slow, barely tugging, but it tickled at the backs of her knees. She teetered up the far bank, hopping from rock to rock. Finally she thumped up the back steps of Sasha and Beanie's cabin. It was the only one on the property that people permanently occupied.

Getting on her tiptoes, Mattie peeked through the windowpanes of the back door. Mr. and Mrs. Little were probably out at the entrance kiosk, but Beanie was inside, dancing on the bench by the kitchen table. Over the soft campground sounds of crackling fires and clinking coffee pots, Mattie could hear her singing.

Through the door. *Way* off all the keys.

Mattie grinned and twisted the knob of the stubborn back door. "Morning, Beanie," she shouted over the blaring music and Beanie's awful singing. She plunked the donut bag down on the kitchen table, which was covered in newspapers and mail, cereal bowls and juice glasses, coloring pages and a half-glued kite.

"Did you bring the good ones?" Beanie asked, jumping down from the kitchen bench. She gave one more little shimmy to the music and pushed her nose into the crumpled paper bag. "Yessss!"

Beanie lined up both chocolate donuts on the edge of the table. She put her nose super close, sizing them up. She'd want the one with the most sprinkles. But no matter which donut Beanie picked, Sasha would always claim to have gotten more sprinkles than her sister, because she could count that high and Beanie couldn't yet. Not without getting the numbers all mixed up.

Beanie picked up her chosen donut, holding it high for one last look before taking a huge, triumphant bite. With her free hand, she pushed Mattie toward the room she shared with her sister.

"Go wake Sasha up. Dad says that after 9:30, we're late!"

"Nah-uh," Mattie said. "You wake her up. She's not my sister."

Messing with Sasha's sleep was kind of a risk.

Beanie gave Mattie a no-way-not-ever look, and Mattie gave in. If she made Beanie wake Sasha up, and then Beanie was too loud or too silly or too *anything*, the morning could turn into kind of a catastrophe.

"Fine," Mattie said, picking up the second place donut to offer to Sasha. It's really hard to be grumpy when you're eating a donut. Even right after someone wakes you up.

Mattie slunk down the hall and into Beanie and Sasha's cozy bedroom. The wooden dresser oozed leggings and shirts, like it had a summer cold and the girls' clothes were boogers. Books dangled from shelves, and the floor was an obstacle course of toys. Somewhere, Mattie was sure, a forgotten orange was going moldy. Mrs. Little hadn't gone on a cleaning rampage in a while.

Sasha was asleep in the room's top bunk, letting out a stuffy-nosed rattle of a snore. One arm was draped over her eyes, keeping out the summer sunshine. Mattie climbed the ladder on the long side of the bunk, next to Sasha's head, holding the donut carefully in one hand. She made sure its chocolate icing didn't get smushed and not a single sprinkle fell off.

She peeked over the edge, watching Sasha sleep.

She nudged at Sasha's elbow.

Nothing.

She blew at the wavy hair plastered to Sasha's forehead.

Snort!

"Sasha," whispered Mattie. "I brought you a donut."

Sasha moaned and turned onto her side.

"Okay . . . I'll go see if Beanie wants it," Mattie said, hopping down a rung.

Sasha flung her arm aside, whapping Mattie on the head.

"Ouch!"

Sasha heaved herself up and plucked the donut from Mattie's hand. "Sorry, Matt. But you know better." She giggled, and Mattie half-smiled back.

Sasha slumped down her bunk ladder, shoved her feet into water shoes, and marched out into the hall. "S'go! We're gonna be late for work."

Mattie followed, listening to Beanie and Sasha's inevitable argument in the kitchen.

"How many did yours have, kid?"

"Two hundred and . . ." Beanie's voice trailed off.

"Too bad, 'cause mine had exactly three hundred and four."

"No way!" Beanie squeaked. "You didn't have time to count that high. Dad says you're always just teasing me."

Mattie sighed. She should just stop bringing them donuts.

"Who are you gonna believe? Dad or me?" Sasha asked, pointing to herself before taking a bite of her donut. "Now let's go," she said, still in her pajamas. "You're always making me late!"

Beanie followed her sister, and Mattie trailed down the stairs behind them, hiding a squished smile. Beanie didn't like it when you laughed at her. Mattie wondered, just for a second, what would have happened if that owl had woken *her* up in the middle of the night!

She couldn't help but giggle at that. No one would have believed Beanie either, and no way would that have been okay with Beanie.

"What?" Beanie peeked back at Mattie.

"Nothing," Mattie said, still kind of laughing.

Sasha rolled her eyes like she knew exactly what Mattie was trying so hard not to laugh at.

"*No* secrets," Beanie complained. "Mom *said*."

"There's no secret. Promise."

"Pinky?" Beanie asked, holding out her little finger.

"Pinky promise," Mattie said, hooking her finger in Beanie's.

Mrs. Little was pretty serious about the girls not keeping secrets from Beanie. They weren't allowed to leave her out. Ever. So if Mattie wanted to help the Littles with their campground check-ins, which she absolutely did, then she had to keep Beanie happy.

And that owl wasn't *really* a secret. It was just something Mattie hadn't figured out how to explain yet.

Not without messing anything up.

THE TURKEY TALON
A FLUFFY MARZIPAN-AND-RAISIN-FILLED BIG SUR VERSION OF A CLASSIC BEAR CLAW. THESE TURKEYS ARE PRETTY WILD!

Alfred awoke with a flinch of feathers as a car careened around the bend beneath his roost. Screeeech. The car slammed on its brakes and honked at the battered station wagon turning left into Owl's Outstanding Donuts. The summer season, Alfred shivered, could be almost unbearable. Reckless tourists!

Ordinarily he would have grumbled himself back to sleep, but this morning he chose to grumble himself across the wooden platform in the scraggly redwood tree that had become his home. The wooden beams had once housed a pair of nesting eagles, and they had been good enough to leave behind a rather comfortable nest. Alfred extended his long feathery legs and hopped down from the magnificent pile of sticks, positioning himself at the platform's edge. He needed a better view of the highway.

Met with the bright sun, his black pupils contracted to pinpoints—ouch. He closed his eyes halfway to keep some of the morning light out.

To his surprise, the ditch where the strange figures had been was not a flurry of human activity. No one was investigating what had occurred the night before. True, there wasn't much to observe, aside from some dark, damp splotches in the gravel. But didn't that dampness give anyone pause? It hadn't rained for weeks. And couldn't people smell that horrible sourness?

Apparently not.

A noisy flock of wild turkeys gobbled its way across the highway. In no rush whatsoever. And as far as Alfred could see, the girl hadn't done a thing about last night's suspicious commotion. He clicked his beak. All his trouble with that flowerpot had come to nothing! And he still had several cactus spines poking around his ankles. Really, besides donuts, what *were* people good for?

Alfred closed his eyes, trying to devise a way, any way, around what he had in mind. Daylight jaunts were beneath his dignity. But he could think of nothing else.

Alfred flew from tree to tree, through the thick forest of redwoods that lined the river. He'd keep to the shadows as he made his way to the Little Family Campground.

Think like a hawk, he counseled himself. Think like a hawk.

He swooped over the riverbed. None of the elderly ladies, up to their ankles in the water, gave him the slightest glance. Excellent.

Alfred landed on the limb of a sycamore and pressed himself against the mottled gray bark.

Then, just below the sycamore, he spotted the girl with green eyes.

But she was with two other humans. Also girls. A tall one and a wiggly one. The tall one held a clipboard and walked ahead of a lurching van. The wiggly one and the girl with green eyes were pointing to an empty campsite. Once the van had come to a halt, the tall one began spouting off a list of campground rules, while the girl with green eyes patiently answered questions about bathrooms and trash. The wiggly one just bounced up and down.

That fledgling was clearly too young, Alfred huffed, to be of any practical use.

Alfred considered the three girls through narrowed eyelids. He knew that children sometimes did unpleasant things like throw stones or pinecones upon seeing an owl. Horrible! But the green-eyed girl didn't strike him as capable of those things.

Now how would he get her alone?

Mattie rocked up onto the tips of her toes. Mr. Little always said the girls should look right into a camper's eyes when they were working, and Mattie could pretty much do it as long as the customer was even a little bit nice back. The woman smiled, and pretty freckles sprinkled her nose, but her breath smelled like coffee and the baby she was bouncing up and down smelled like . . . something else. Mattie decided to focus on the smile and not breathe too deeply while her nose was near the baby's diaper.

"Here's your car pass," Mattie said, handing over a little pink ticket. "Just come to the kiosk if you have any more questions."

"Yep," squeaked Beanie.

"Let's see if we can break the record today," Sasha said, already zooming up the road that snaked through the campground. "Think we can do twenty-one check-ins?"

Mattie was about to remind Sasha that the day they did twenty-one check-ins for Mr. and Mrs. Little, Mrs. Little had told them they shouldn't rush the process. If they did, they might forget some of the things they were supposed to tell the customers, and anyway, camping was supposed to be relaxing. But the only time Sasha ever relaxed was when she was asleep or reading a book.

Sasha was the only one who really cared about their record. Mattie tried to think of a way to remind Sasha that they weren't supposed to speed through good customer service—without Sasha getting mad—when a shadow flickered over her. But when she looked up, all she saw was an empty sycamore branch.

She shook her head and hurried after the sisters.

Back at the entrance kiosk, a couple of cars were lined up behind the striped brown-and-white gate. Mattie, Sasha, and Beanie hopped up onto the bench outside the kiosk window and poked their heads inside for their next assignment. Every surface inside the tiny building burst with trail maps, chips, granola bars, lip balm, sunscreen, disposable cameras, marshmallow roasters, fire starters, and water shoes. Basically everything campers might need and would probably pay double for just so they didn't have to drive to a store.

Mr. Little was chatting with a man leaning out of his car window when Adelaide Sharpe's shiny red car pulled into a visitor parking space. Mr. Little leaned back into the kiosk. "Sharpe's here again," he said to Mrs. Little.

"Make sure she buys something," Mrs. Little called back. "Just not the campsite."

Mattie giggled. The real estate agent must have been pestering everyone with a driveway off Highway One.

Mrs. Little was tucked away in the corner, looking up reservations on the computer and calling out campsite numbers. She stopped typing every few seconds to take a nibble from a Turkey Talon donut. Turkey Talons were Mrs. Little's favorite, which was one of the reasons that Mattie knew Mrs. Little wasn't as tough as she pretended to be.

"We finished with site twenty-seven," Sasha shouted, interrupting her dad.

Mr. Little passed a form to the guy in the car, not answering. When the visitor signed the paper and handed it back, Mr. Little ripped off the top sheet and passed it to Sasha, who added it to her clipboard. Then he gave another little pink parking pass to Mattie and a high five to Beanie just because she was so cute.

"These three turkeys of mine will show you where to park!" Mr. Little said.

Mattie was relieved to have a job to do instead of watching Adelaide Sharpe teeter her way across the potholed driveway. But she did wonder what Mr. Little would convince Sharpe to buy from the crammed-full camp shop.

Mattie and the sisters scuttled down off the bench and stood in front of the automatic gate. The girls had a three-part job when they helped Mr. and Mrs. Little. Taking the campers to the right spot, making sure they used their parking pass, and answering questions.

"This way to site thirty-two," Mattie said, as the gate squeaked up into the air.

Two check-ins later, the girls were hustling their way back to the kiosk when Mattie saw Mrs. Mantooth speed-walking down one of the campground lanes.

"Great," she grumbled.

Even though Mrs. Mantooth hated it when people backed their cars *two feet* into *her* gravel driveway, she seemed to think the whole county belonged to her. Mattie wished that Mrs. Little would tell her to stop using the campground for her power walks, but Mrs. Little was too smart to get on Mrs. Mantooth's bad side.

Most days, Mrs. Mantooth at least kept to herself. But that day, she swish-walked right up to the girls.

"Morning, Mrs. Mantooth," Mattie said.

Mrs. Mantooth started straight in. "Mattie, tell your aunt that the well water's been tasting funny. It has a definite odor. Sulfurous. She needs to be more watchful about contaminants, especially with a young girl like you around. You're growing!"

She poked at Mattie's shoulder with one finger.

It kind of hurt.

"Okay, Mrs. Mantooth," Mattie said. "I'll tell her, but I haven't noticed anything."

Satisfied, Mrs. Mantooth executed a perfect turn and speed-walked back where she came from. Mrs. Mantooth was relentless about wanting improvements on the well, but her reason for wanting them was always a little different. There was sulfur, there was salt, the pump was creaky, the pump was slow, the well should be deeper, or the pipes were too old. So Mattie was one-hundred-percent not going to tell Aunt Molly about Mrs. Mantooth's latest complaint.

"Can we get back on track?" Sasha said.

"Yes, *please*," said Mattie.

Beanie giggled.

Three campsites later and twelve away from beating their record, Mattie couldn't shake the feeling that something was following her around. Something besides pesky neighbors or lurchy cars lined up to check in. But every time she turned her head, there wasn't anything to see. Until a funny shadow snuck over her arm. When she looked up this time, she spotted it.

That owl!

It was almost perfectly camouflaged against the bark of a big sycamore, all gray and speckled white. Although its beak wasn't smeared with pink icing anymore.

The owl blinked its big orange eyes at her. It didn't hoot, but Mattie was pretty sure it was waiting for something. And one-hundred-percent sure it was watching her.

"Sasha," she whispered. "Look!"

Mattie pointed at the owl, and the bird closed its eyes, which made it almost disappear against the tree.

"What? Where? What?" Beanie said, hopping up and down.

"It's an owl," Mattie said.

Beanie stared up into the tree. "I don't see it."

Sasha looked too, wrinkling her nose. "There's nothing there. It probably just flew off or something. And no way was it an owl—they only come out at night. Maybe a hawk. Come on—let's go!"

But Mattie didn't move. She could still see the outline of the owl if she squinted just right. And once Sasha and Beanie started heading back to the kiosk, the owl opened its eyes again, giving the sycamore two little gold polka dots halfway up its trunk.

Mattie sucked in a breath.

She kind of wanted to say hi.

But before she could, the owl lifted its talons off the branch and dropped something. A dark clump landed in the dirt at the edge of the gravel road with a squelchy little thump.

Mattie muttered Aunt Molly's favorite exclamation: "What in the donut hole?"

Beanie and Sasha were already halfway back to the entrance kiosk, so she ran across the campground lane by herself. But when she looked up, the owl was gone.

Mattie bent over the dark gloppy mass of . . . what? She slid to one knee and peeked closer. The clump had bits of damp gravel and dirt, held together by something slimy and dark.

Mattie sniffed.

Whatever that sticky goop was, it sure didn't smell very nice. She didn't want to touch it. But she couldn't ignore it either. She peeked into a campground trashcan and pulled out a mostly clean-looking plastic bag.

She turned the bag inside out, shook out what she was pretty sure were old graham cracker crumbs, and picked up the clump of goop. Carefully, without touching it even once.

What the heck was it?

And why did that owl keep following her around?

Mattie was supposed to understand something or

do something. She knew that. But what? Asking Aunt Molly was out of bounds. No way was she risking school over an owl and some mysterious goo. So she ran to catch up with Sasha and Beanie. She'd changed her mind again.

THE GOLDEN GALAXY
A CINNAMON AND TOASTED CARDAMOM INFUSED CAKE DONUT, ICED WITH A DECADENT DARK CHOCOLATE GLAZE, AND TOPPED WITH GLITTERY GOLD LEAF

"Wait!" Mattie called to the girls.

They stopped by the camping grounds' empty basketball court so Mattie could catch up. Sasha folded her arms and tapped her foot. Beanie picked up a battered hula-hoop and swung it around her waist. It swish-rattle-swished while Mattie tried to explain.

"We've got to go check something out," Mattie said, peeking around to see if anyone else was close enough to hear. "Something weird happened last night and—"

"I knew you had a secret!" Beanie scowled, but she never let the hula-hoop stop its orbit. Swish-rattle-swish.

Sasha shook her head. "No way, Mattie. We're on track to beat my record today. No more distractions!"

"Just listen," Mattie said.

Sasha sighed, but it sounded more like a mad cat hiss. "Fine. What?"

"So . . . last night, an owl—"

"What kind?" Sasha asked.

"I don't know. The big hooty kind."

"Great horned," said Sasha.

"Okay, so last night, this great horned owl basically knocked on my window and woke me up and maybe smashed a flowerpot to get my attention."

Beanie's hula-hoop clattered to the asphalt. Sasha just rolled her eyes. But both she and Beanie listened while Mattie told the whole story about the owl, the truck, the flying flowerpot, and the clue. That's what Mattie called the bag of goopy gravel, because that's what she thought it was. She handed it over to Beanie, and Beanie's eyes went all shiny like glazed donuts.

"Gloop!" Beanie said, holding the bag inches from her eyeballs.

At least Beanie believed her, Mattie thought, sneaking a sideways look at Sasha.

Sasha pushed her short blond hair behind her ears. "That is the weirdest thing I have ever heard," said Sasha. "Owls don't come out during the day. She's just kidding, Beanie." She glared at Mattie. "We're wasting too much time."

"I'm not kidding," Mattie said. "Super-honest swear. This isn't a story. Come on, we have to at least check out the scene. I think that truck was up to something last night."

Beanie bounced up and down, flopping the bag of gloop around. "Check it out, check it out, check it out!"

"Let's get this over with," Sasha said.

Mattie smiled. Just a little. Convincing Sasha to change her plan for the day wasn't something anybody else could do. Except for maybe Mrs. Little, who said that she had executive authority, which meant that she was the boss of everyone. Even Sasha.

Mattie grabbed the clue from Beanie and hid it in the pocket of her shorts. Then the girls told Mr. Little they were taking their lunch break early. They splunked up the river to Mattie's place. All the way there, under the rope bridge, up the stone steps in the bank, down the path that curved around the trailer, and across the donut shop parking lot, Sasha led the way.

"Where was it?" Sasha asked.

Mattie pointed to where she'd seen the mystery truck parked: the gravel shoulder on the far side of the highway. "There," she said, feeling serious and queasy.

As the three of them reached the nearest edge of the black road, Mattie hesitated. Her nightmares might have stopped, but just being near the highway and all its whooshing cars made Mattie feel like she'd just woken up after the dream's final crunch. Sweaty-cold and scared. She'd told herself for weeks that riding the school bus in September was going to be okay, but being so close to cars speeding down the highway made that feel like a lie.

Sasha looked left and right. All three of them listened for the echoing swoosh of another car on the way. Mattie's heart did a butterfly flip-flop.

"Ready?" Sasha said when the coast was clear.

"Let's go!" Beanie said.

Mattie didn't answer and she definitely didn't go. Sasha grabbed her hand.

"Hold on to Mattie's other one, Beanie," Sasha said, like she was worried that Beanie would wander off like a baby turkey as they crossed the highway. Pretending like she was doing it because she was Beanie's big sister and not to help Mattie.

Then the three of them darted across the road, which no way were they ever supposed to do, and jumped into a ditch beyond the gravel shoulder. Mattie's heart was still doing its wild butterfly flop, but she'd made it.

"Beanie, get off my foot," Sasha said, giving her sister a little push.

Beanie hopped off Sasha's water shoe and slipped on something gooey. "Ewww," Beanie squealed, wiping the bottom of her own shoe on a rock until a plop of something came off, like a giant black booger.

"Don't touch it," Sasha told her.

"I wasn't gonna," Beanie said.

"Look, there's more," Mattie said. "This must be the gloop!"

The ditch ran along the highway like a little creek that only filled up on rainy days. But it hadn't rained all month, maybe even all summer, and the ditch was dry except for the mysterious gloop. The stuff shimmered against the gravel like the fuzzy head of a dead fly.

Mattie followed a trail of stinky black slime down the ditch, past a sloppy puddle, and all the way to a pipe with a grate over it.

"I bet most of it went down here," Mattie said. Her voice echoed in the metal tunnel, and her heart thudded like thunder.

She knew where that pipe went.

It ran straight under the highway, with water flowing from the ditch into the Big Sur River, just upstream from the donut shop. Right where a little creek forked off from the river. And that creek dumped straight into the ocean. Mattie had followed it down to the pink sands of Pfeiffer Beach last summer. So in a way, everything that flowed out of the ditch didn't just go into river, it went straight into the ocean too. Though late in the summer, Sycamore Creek wasn't more than a trickle, so not much from the ditch would actually reach the Pacific Ocean.

Mattie sniffed.

The gloop had a sourness almost like barf. She coughed. It could be anything. Old milk? A pesticide? A poison?

Some of the slime looked older. Some was all fresh and slippery. Whoever was dumping it had been around more than once.

"This is so bad," Mattie said.

"Gross," Beanie said, sticking her tongue out.

"This is what you dragged me across the highway for?" Sasha said. "It just looks like some jerk from the city emptied out their sludgy cooler water at the side of the road. Dad keeps telling them not to do it in the camp."

Beanie looked up at Mattie, waiting to see what *she* thought.

"This doesn't look like cooler sludge to me," Mattie said. "There's way too much for that. It's all over the place. And it stinks. And it looks like it went into that pipe! That flows into the river *and* the creek *and* the ocean. We're lucky it hasn't rained, or the stuff would have made it there already. What if they come back again and dump some more?"

"Why would they come back?" Sasha said. "That doesn't make any sense. Those LA jerks are long gone."

"I don't think so. Look, some of the gloop is all dried and crusty. Some of it is still super slimy. It's like there are two trails. Maybe even three. I don't think those guys are finished. And . . . that owl doesn't think so either. I know it. Why else would he leave me a clue?"

Sasha shook her head. "An *owl* didn't leave you a clue, Matt. That's impossible."

Mattie pulled the plastic bag of gloopy gravel out of her pocket again. "But . . . look. It's a perfect match. Same color. Same gravel. Same smell. When I found it, there were even talon marks in the gloop."

"Even if that's true—if you saw an owl in the *middle of the day*, and some gunk fell off its feet—it didn't do that on purpose," Sasha said.

Mattie held the gloop bag up between them. It swung in the air. "It absolutely, totally, one-hundred-percent *did*."

Beanie's eyes bugged out at all the amazing mysteriousness.

"Let's be detectives," she said, bouncing a little.

Mattie nodded. "Good idea, Beanie. You know what we need to do? We need to do a stakeout."

"Yessss!" Beanie said, bouncing higher.

"A sleepover stakeout," Mattie said, peeking at Sasha.

Mattie could tell Sasha wasn't convinced, but she was pretty sure even Sasha wouldn't say no to a sleepover. Sasha huffed, which meant maybe, and maybe probably meant yes.

"Come on, Beanie," Sasha said, grabbing her sister's hand. "We've got to have lunch and get back to work or Mom will be suspicious."

She tugged Beanie up to the road, looked both ways, listened, and ran for it with Beanie bouncing at the end of her arm.

Mattie just stood there in the ditch.

By herself.

That trail of shiny ooze looked like something an enormous mutant banana slug had left in the ditch after slithering its way into the pipe. Mattie was tempted to follow the ooze through the pipe and toward the creek, but what if that took her all the way down to the beach? That would mean she'd be gone almost the whole day. And she still didn't want Aunt Molly getting suspicious.

A gust of wind sent the forest of redwood trees shivering. Mattie shoved the bag of gloop back into her pocket and scrambled up the steep ditch. She flinched at the edge of the road. Sasha and Beanie were already on the far end of the parking lot. She held her breath, listening. No cars in sight. No whoosh of one coming through the trees. She zipped across the highway with her heart thudding.

That gloop was suddenly scarier than her old dream.

What if it did get all the way down to the ocean? What if it seeped down into the well they shared with Mrs. Mantooth? The well barely went down thirty feet and was super close to the riverbank. What if the gloop was in their water already?

That was something Mattie didn't even want to think about. Mrs. Mantooth would go berserk for sure. She wouldn't just want a new pump. She'd want a new everything. Which no way could Aunt Molly afford.

Mattie had to keep the gloop a secret . . . until she caught those guys in the act. She needed proof that it was someone else's fault. Otherwise, Mrs. Mantooth was guaranteed to make trouble for Aunt Molly. Then what would happen to the donut shop and their trailer?

"Sleepover?" Mattie yelled, her heart still thudding.

"Maybe," Sasha said over her shoulder. "After work." And she tugged Beanie out of sight.

Mattie ran off to Owl's, her brain buzzing with a plan, listing off all the things she'd need to do if she wanted to bust the gloop culprits. She'd find out what was going on.

Aunt Molly was at the back counter, putting the finishing touches on a tray of Golden Galaxies. Martín was manning the cash register.

He winked and Mattie smiled.

Martín didn't really like donuts. Not that Mattie could tell. He would get a couple dozen when his nephew had a birthday or when he had a family party to go to. Mattie liked watching him smile while he loaded Chocolate Rainbows or Slug Bars into pink boxes. He was the kind of person who liked to bring *other people* donuts, and that was one of Mattie's favorite kinds of people.

Behind Martín, Aunt Molly's arms were covered in flecks of gold leaf from the Galaxies—they were the hardest to glaze—but she was all happy and hummy, with her back to the shop. Good. Aunt Molly couldn't have seen her crossing the road.

"Can we have a sleepover tonight?" Mattie asked, slipping behind the counter. "Me and Sasha and Beanie?"

Aunt Molly wiped her hands on a dishtowel, sending little gold flakes shimmering to the ground. "Are you sure a sleepover is a good idea? What about your bad dreams?"

Mattie snuck a look at Martín, and he turned away,

pretending that the milk cartons in the fridge needed reorganizing.

"It wasn't . . . I'm not . . . I'll be fine. Please?" Mattie asked.

"All right. Okay. I'll call Mrs. Little." Aunt Molly nodded to herself. It was like she had agreed but still didn't think it was a great idea.

Mattie grinned, forgetting for a second that this wasn't going to be just any sleepover.

"But before I do," Aunt Molly said, "can you put this tray in the case?" She pointed to the finished donuts. "And I set your lunch out on the table at home."

Mattie nodded super-fast. "Got it!"

Aunt Molly gave Mattie one more long look before she hustled off into the back room, mumbling a recipe under her breath.

Mattie picked up the big tray of Golden Galaxies and slid them into the display case. The shiny gold circles flashed in the sunlight coming from the front windows. Mattie thought again about owl eyes flashing from the sycamore tree that morning. But the shiny circles made her think of her mom too. The gold-leaf donuts had been Mom's idea. She loved fancy things.

Mattie tried to clear that thought from her brain, like she was wiping down a counter. Thinking about Mom in the middle of the day was a recipe for disaster.

"Martín?"

"¿Qué pasa?" he answered.

"How do you say *owl* in Spanish?"

"In El Salvador, we say 'tecolote,'" Martín said. "How come?"

Mattie stared at the Galaxies and closed the case nice and slow. A cloud-shaped shadow traveled across the whole shop, making the sunny owl-eye donuts in the display case seem to wink and blink at her.

"I'm not really sure," she said to Martín. "Not yet." And then she practiced the new word under her breath. "Tecolote. Tecolote. Tecolote."

THE DONUT HOLE
WHERE DOES THE MIDDLE OF A DONUT GO? LOOK NO
FURTHER. HERE THEY ARE. ASSORTED DONUT HOLES ARE
GLAZED AND FLAVORED DAILY AS THE MOOD STRIKES.
WATCH OUT FOR STRAY SPRINKLES!

The lunch that Aunt Molly had left on the table in the trailer was a giant pita sandwich stuffed with fried falafel and crunchy cucumbers. It dripped with homemade hummus and a tangy cumin yogurt sauce. Mattie made a mess when she ate, but only when nobody was looking.

Crunch.

Drip.

Plop.

Yum!

Aunt Molly's food, not just her donuts, was one of the things that Mattie wasn't sure she should like so much without her mom around. Aunt Molly cooked lentil soup and coconut rice, salty hot focaccia bread with herbs, and homemade macaroni with bubbly cheese. She had about a million different recipes for quiche too.

Mom just used to get a lot of stuff from the takeout deli in Monterey.

Cooking was something that Mom and Aunt Molly had always joked about. When Grandma left the donut shop to both sisters, it was pretty obvious to everybody who the new baker was going to be. Besides, Mattie knew that as much as her mom loved visiting her sister in Big Sur and eating Aunt Molly's food, she never wanted to live there.

But whenever Mattie and Mom had visited Aunt Molly's little trailer, Mattie thought it was perfect. The Airstream didn't ever go anywhere, but it *could*. That's what Aunt Molly and Grandma always said. It had everything a person could need. And even though the big wooden deck that Grandpa had built around the trailer was pretty permanent, the *idea* of freedom had helped Aunt Molly feel at home there.

Mattie liked that her aunt's trailer was a place you couldn't lose things in. And she never felt alone there, even when she was by herself. But whenever she started to feel good about that, she felt guilty right afterward.

Mattie crunched the last bite of her falafel sandwich and licked her fingers. Next, she clumped out onto the trailer deck and stared across the road, puzzling out the giant trail of slime they'd found. She couldn't see it from the deck. Nobody could see it, unless they were looking right into the ditch. The gloop had to have come from that truck. But what *was* it?

If she could catch those guys in the act and prove to Aunt Molly what was going on, then she'd be able to call the sheriff's department. Aunt Molly said she shouldn't bother them, but without any proof like a picture or a license plate number, maybe the sheriff wouldn't be able to help anyway. They'd never caught the person who ran Mattie's mom off the road, even though witnesses had seen the other car. Even though there were black tire marks where the driver had crossed the double lines.

Mattie needed to wait for the culprits to come back. When they did, she'd be ready. Patience wasn't something she had trouble with.

A flutter moved through the cypress trees hanging over the deck. Mattie caught her breath. But it wasn't an owl. Instead, something blue flashed in the shadows. Mattie unscrewed the Mason jar full of peanuts that was always sitting on the deck rail and balanced one peanut in her palm.

Leaning against the wood, she waited.

Then, swoop, down from the trees, a Steller's jay landed on the railing. The bright blue bird with a tall crown of feathers cocked its head, giving Mattie the eye. Mattie stared right back and held the peanut perfectly still.

Hop.

The bird bounced closer.

Patient.

Still.

Hop.

It landed right on her fingertips and snatched the peanut up.

The jay zoomed away, and the burst of air from its wings tickled Mattie's cheeks. The neighborhood birds were smart. By the time the first one had retreated to hide its peanut, three more had perched in the cypress trees. When they looked at Mattie, she could tell they recognized her. But they were still just normal birds. They didn't drop clues or throw flowerpots.

That owl was different.

Mattie was *sure*, and she was going to find out why.

The afternoon stretched into evening, and the shadows of trees crept across the parking lot while Mattie watched from the deck. The peanut jar was half empty when she went back inside the trailer.

Were Beanie and Sasha really going to come for the sleepover?

She had everything ready, but she wasn't so sure about Sasha's maybe being a yes anymore. Aunt Molly had made the dough for tiny personal pizzas on her afternoon break, which the girls would decorate together with olives and vegetarian pepperonis . . . *if* Sasha and Beanie came.

Mattie had charged up Aunt Molly's old phone. She was allowed to use it to play games and listen to audio books, because Aunt Molly had a shiny new one. That old phone couldn't call anybody. The screen was cracked down the middle, and the battery would barely last an hour. But the phone's camera could still take pictures and videos—Mattie double-checked. She'd put fresh batteries in her pink flashlight too, and written down everything she could remember about the night before in a little spiral notebook, just like she was a real detective. She'd even transferred the plastic bag of gloop to an old jam jar and put it on her shelf next to the container of pink sand she'd collected at Pfeiffer Beach the summer before.

She was ready for the stakeout.

Even if it was just going to be her.

When the door of the trailer boomed with a series of knocks, bang-bunk-boof, Mattie almost jumped off the couch.

"Coming, Beanie," Mattie said, leaping for the door.

Mattie flung the door open, and there Beanie was, buried behind two sleeping bags and carrying an overstuffed backpack. She must have used her foot to knock. Mattie checked the path behind her. "Where's Sasha?"

Mattie couldn't understand Beanie's muffled reply. The sleeping bags were completely covering her mouth.

Mattie giggled and grabbed the bags, tossing them into the trailer. "I said, where's Sasha?"

"I'm right here, birdbrain," Sasha said. She walked up the deck steps with her empty arms crossed.

Beanie hustled around Mattie and stretched out face down on the little purple velvet couch, still wearing her overstuffed backpack.

Sasha slid into the trailer like a cat. Mattie was just about to say something about the birdbrain crack—even her patience had limits—when Sasha let this twinkly excited look sneak out of her eyes. So Mattie knew that Sasha had believed her about the whole owl-flowerpot-truck thing. At least a little bit.

"Let's get this stakeout started," Sasha said, certain that nothing important could start without her saying so. "I call the couch."

"Awww," Beanie groaned. "You always call the couch. I got here first."

"Don't worry, Beanie," Mattie smiled. "You can sleep with me."

The first part of the sleepover stakeout went perfect. Beanie made a smiley face out of the olives and fake pepperonis on her pizza. Sasha made a perfect grid so that every bite would have just the right amount of tastiness. Mattie kept hers pretty simple. Cheese. Cheese. And more cheese.

Aunt Molly came home on the early side, since it was Martín's night to lock up. She brought a jumble of donut holes for everybody to share. When it came to Mattie and her friends, Aunt Molly had three rules about donuts: they were for Sunday mornings, birthdays, and sleepovers. Mattie thought donut holes were the happiest kind of donut. Sometimes they were plain, nothing fancy, but it was like they were meant for sleepovers.

Once Aunt Molly went off to her tiny room and closed the curtain, a slimy seriousness settled over the girls. Sort of. There was still plenty of giggling and shining flashlights in each other's eyes, and Beanie brought out her joke book. But they all took turns at the window. Waiting for that truck to come back. Waiting for that owl to show itself. Waiting for flying flowerpots.

When they got down to the last donut hole, Beanie and Sasha started arguing over who would get it. So Mattie snuck outside and put it on the edge of the flowerbox outside her window.

For the owl.

(It had strawberry icing.)

While Mattie was outside, she saw the donut shop sign flicker off across the parking lot. Martín left through the back door, threw a bag of trash into the dumpster, and drove off in his old blue Civic. Mattie sighed, hoping that Beanie and Sasha were ready to be patient during the long night ahead of them, and slipped back into the trailer.

"Last night it was *really* late when those people in the truck came," Mattie told the sisters.

"The *gloop* truck," Beanie said, shining a flashlight under her chin and trying to make a scary face.

Sasha pulled her knees closer to her, making a little tent with her sleeping bag. She was still sitting up on the couch, but she already looked tired, red eyed, and annoyed.

"Beanie, read us some jokes to keep us awake," Mattie suggested, hopping into bed.

Beanie lunged for the dictionary-sized copy of her favorite book and flipped through the pages like an excited puppy.

"There's a whole section on owl jokes. Ready?"

Beanie didn't wait for either of the other girls to answer. She barreled into the book using her patented joke voice. "What do you call an owl magician?"

"What?" Mattie asked, even though she knew.

"Whoo-dini," Sasha said. "Everybody knows that one, Beanie. Find something funny."

Beanie bounced up on her knees with her hands up. "Okay. Okay . . . Did you hear the one about the owl?"

"No," Mattie said.

"Yes," Sasha said, trying to hide her smile.

"It's a real hoot!" Beanie said the punch line with a little wiggle, and this time even Sasha laughed.

But an hour and a half later, Beanie had made it through all of the owl section, and all of the opossum, porcupine, and peacock sections too. There was no sign of a mysterious truck and definitely no sign of a flowerpot-flinging owl.

Sasha got grouchier and grouchier as the night got longer. She wasn't the kind of kid who could stay up all night and share jokes.

"See, I told you she was lying," Sasha said to Beanie. "I'm going to sleep. This stakeout is over. Only regular sleepovers from now on." She pulled the sleeping bag over her head, rolled onto her side, and clicked off her flashlight.

Mattie stared out her window and across the highway, wishing for something to happen, even though she knew that something could be bad. Beanie gave a sleepy sigh, flipping back to the owl section of her joke book.

"Knock-knock," she said.

"Who's there?" whispered Mattie.

"Owls."

"Owls, who?"

"Why yes they do," Beanie said a little too loud.

"Beannieeeeeee, knock it off," Sasha hissed from deep inside her sleeping bag.

"Did you say knock-knock?" Beanie said.

"I mean it, Beanie. Be quiet. That owl isn't coming."

Beanie didn't tell any more jokes. Five minutes later, she was snoring on Mattie's side of the bed. Mattie leaned her head against her window and clicked off her light. Three cars whooshed past the gloopy bend in the road. One red. Two blue. No white truck. Mattie closed her eyes.

Alfred hopped from foot to foot, digging his claws into the old eagle perch as he watched Mattie fall asleep with her cheek pressed against the window.

Well, really, Alfred thought. The green-eyed girl certainly wasn't much of a night owl.

He dove in a graceful arc toward the donut shop dumpster. He thought there might be another strawberry donut in its depths and hoped this one wouldn't have too many sprinkles. But when he landed on the metal lid, he found no clear way to enter the container. The last man to leave the shop had closed everything up too tightly.

There was such a thing, Alfred thought, as a job too well done.

He shivered and took flight, circling above the empty parking lot once more. A dot of pink caught his eye. Alfred swerved and landed rather ungracefully in the flowerbox outside of Mattie's window.

Among the damp flowers, he discovered the last donut hole.

It had strawberry icing!

Clacking his beak, Alfred gobbled it up. The girl was no night owl, he thought, but she had excellent taste.

Alfred felt the smallest glimmer of guilt. The girl would lose even more sleep after what he was about to do. But hadn't he been about in broad daylight just that morning? He'd lost hours of rest. And he couldn't let Mattie drop her guard.

"Whooo-whoo-whoo," Alfred hooted with his beak directly across from the sleeping girl's nose. His hooting had the desired effect. It fogged the window nicely, and she opened her green eyes with a start.

Carefully, tottering on one feathery foot, Alfred traced something into the flowerbed with his talon.

Two short, and somewhat crooked, lines.

Mattie rubbed her eyes and stared at the crooked little lines. She pulled Aunt Molly's old phone from her pajama pocket and took a picture before anything could disturb the dirt.

"Wait there," she whispered as the owl hopped from the trailer's window box to the deck railing with its wings outstretched. Before the bird could go any farther, Mattie looked down at the screen of Aunt Molly's phone.

She frowned. In Mattie's picture, the owl stood balanced with one foot gripping the wooden edge of the box. Its other foot was a blur of curved talons at the edge of the photo, and the crooked lines in the dirt didn't show up all that well. Still, even if finding those marks wasn't the same as catching the gloop truck in the act, she was sure they were another clue.

When she looked back up, the owl took off with a silent swoop toward the cypress trees above the trailer.

Mattie hopped across a sleeping Beanie, landed with a soft thud, and tiptoed to the purple couch. She shook Sasha awake. "The owl's back," she whispered. "Come on."

She snuck to the trailer door, turned the handle slow

so it wouldn't creak, and slipped out onto the deck. The frogs were going wild down in the river, and crickets chirped from the bushes. Mattie didn't hear any hooting.

Sasha crept out onto the deck with a pretty irritated look on her face. "So, where is it?"

Mattie put her finger to her lips, so Sasha would whisper.

She craned her neck, checking the cypress trees that leaned over the deck. But she didn't see the owl.

"I think it's gone," she said. "But it left another clue, and look! It ate the donut hole I left in the window box."

"Clue?" Sasha said, with a gravely half-asleep voice. "What clue?"

"It hooted right against the window and then it drew these two lines in the flowerbox dirt," Mattie said, pointing.

Sasha didn't look so convinced about those two lines.

And without the owl in the window box, the marks did kind of just look like . . . dirt.

Before Mattie could show Sasha the blurry picture she'd taken, Sasha was back in the trailer, stuffing her sleeping bag into its sack and muttering about everybody keeping her awake for nothing.

"I'm going home. I can't sleep here. This is stupid."

Sasha clicked on her flashlight, left the trailer for the last time, and stomped down the steps. Mattie was sure her friend's cranky footsteps would wake Aunt Molly, but they didn't.

Mattie wanted to shout at Sasha to come back and stay, shout about her proof, but that would mean waking Aunt Molly up for sure. Sasha's light bounced off the trees nearby, and Mattie heard the frogs go quiet as Sasha sloshed through the river. She sighed, hoping that Sasha would calm down on her own. She usually did. Mattie could show her the picture in the morning.

She tiptoed over to the window box. The donut really was gone, and when she studied the dirt with her flashlight, she found a few perfect talon prints in the potting soil around the two crooked lines. Beanie was still snoring, sprawled sideways in Mattie's bed. Mattie tapped on the window from the outside, and Beanie woke with a snort, looking one-hundred-percent awake.

She scrambled outside.

"Did the truck come?" Beanie shout-whispered.

"Nope," Mattie said. "Not the truck, but . . . somebody came."

Beanie's mouth plopped open. "Who?"

"*Whoooooo* do you think?" Mattie said.

Mattie pointed to the window box. "The truck didn't come, but the owl came and did this."

She leaned close to the window box, with Beanie teetering on her tiptoes beside her. "See the owl tracks?" Mattie traced the outlines of the three-taloned prints. "And look, the owl drew two little lines in the dirt before it flew away. They're a message!"

"Whoa!" Beanie said. "What do they mean?"

"I don't know," Mattie said, shrugging her shoulders. "It's got to be a clue, though."

"*Got* to be," said Beanie, bopping her head yes.

Mattie took more pictures, trying to capture the talon prints and lines in the window box too. But those didn't really come out either. Not even when she shined her flashlight on them. She stared into the trees, hoping to see the owl again, but she couldn't spot him in the dark. So she hustled Beanie inside and closed the door without creaking it. Beanie didn't even ask about Sasha, and she was back asleep before the frogs were singing again. Mattie fell asleep listening to the crickets and the tree frogs. They gave a rhythm to the puzzle she turned over and over in her brain.

Two little lines. Two little lines. Two little . . .

THE BANANA BOAT
BITE SIZED BANANA FRITTERS DRIPPING WITH ORANGE-BLOSSOM HONEY SYRUP AND SERVED PIPING HOT WITH A GENEROUS DOLLOP OF TANGERINE WHIPPED CREAM

Monday morning, Mattie and Beanie slept late. It was already hot in the trailer when Mattie threw the covers off. She jiggled Beanie awake.

"Where's Sasha?" Beanie asked, staring at the empty couch and rubbing the crust from her eyes.

Mattie shrugged. "She went home. She was too mad about me waking her up to listen about all the clues last night. Let's get breakfast—we can fill her in later."

Mattie led the way across the parking lot to the donut shop.

Not for donuts.

Aunt Molly was surprisingly strict about sugar for a gourmet donut baker. It wasn't Sunday, they'd already used up their sleepover donuts, and Beanie's birthday wasn't until Wednesday. Besides, only Beanie would get that donut.

Beanie burst though the jingly door and hustled

to her favorite booth. Out-of-town customers smiled at the little girl in rainbow-striped pajamas. Mattie walked by, trying not to attract any extra attention. Aunt Molly pushed the buttons on her cash register, making it click and bing like music. Martín manned the sizzling fryer. Paper bags crackled as Molly dropped donuts inside them. Chairs scooted as people sat up or settled in. Even a Monday was big business at Owl's near the end of the summer. But despite the noise, Mattie's mind felt quiet.

Two. Two, two, two. What did the owl's message mean? There were two scratches. Two lines. Two people by the truck. Mattie wondered if those lines could be an eleven, but she shrugged that idea away. Owls, even amazing ones, probably didn't know how to write.

In a lull between customers, Aunt Molly plopped down next to Mattie and put three warm foil-wrapped breakfast burritos on the table. To make Monday breakfast special, Aunt Molly always traded goodies with the restaurant up the road.

"Morning, Beatrice," Aunt Molly said. "Where's Sasha? Still asleep?"

Beanie, her head half buried in an egg, cheese, and soy sausage burrito, made an indiscernible noise. Aunt Molly laughed.

"What did you say?" Aunt Molly asked.

Beanie wiped her eggy mouth on her wrist. "Sasha woke up grouchy about the—"

Mattie kicked at Beanie's feet under the table and mouthed *no*, so Beanie wouldn't say anything about the owl's newest clue.

Beanie wiggled her eyebrows like she was onto the game and dove back into her breakfast.

"Why don't you take Sasha a burrito?" Aunt Molly asked. "Burritos make everything better. Even not getting enough sleep because your friends were giggling too much."

A new rush of customers crowded through the door. Molly smiled at the girls and swooped back to the register.

Mattie leaned toward Beanie. "You can't say anything about the owl until we have more evidence," she whispered. "Grownups just don't get it."

"Got it," Beanie said.

Mattie munched and wondered about the owl's clue. Two *what*? She had a few ideas, but she wasn't sure about anything. She wished that she could ask the owl just what it meant, but that seemed impossible.

Mattie eyed the newest line of customers. She'd always loved watching the people line up, loved guessing who they were and what they would order, guessing what they were like. It was something she was good at. But now . . . now they could be suspects too. So maybe she wasn't so good at figuring people out after all.

Mattie wanted to think that no *real* customer would dump gloop across the road. Everybody who came into the shop loved Aunt Molly's donuts . . . right? Still,

Mattie was starting to feel sure that the gloopers must have been from nearby. How far would some crook really drive to dump gloop at the side of a road, anyway?

And if they were locals, they could still be hanging around. They could be anybody.

"We should make a list of suspects—you know, do some investigating," she told Beanie.

"We could check all the parking lots for that stinky truck," Beanie said with her mouth full.

Mattie nodded all slow. She didn't think finding the truck would be that easy. Why would sneaks like those gloopers leave such a big clue parked out in the open? But it was *possible*. And looking for the truck would give Beanie something to do while Mattie and Sasha snooped for suspects. *If* she could get Sasha to come along.

Mattie snatched up the last breakfast burrito. "Come on—let's get to work!"

"But it's Monday," said Beanie. "We only do check-ins on the weekend."

"Not campground work, silly. Let's go get Sasha and check out all the parking lots."

Beanie bounced up. "Right! That was *my* idea."

The two girls waved goodbye to Martín and tossed their crumpled balls of burrito foil into the recycling bin. Sasha's burrito was still warm when they got to the Little family cabin, but Sasha wasn't there. Sasha wasn't anywhere. Beanie and Mattie checked the top bunk and the bathroom and the blanket fort in the living room where Sasha liked to hide out and read. They checked the check-in kiosk and the pool and the basketball courts under the redwoods where Sasha liked to sit and watch the visitor kids. They asked Mrs. Little and Mr. Little and a bunch of the campground guests.

Nobody knew where Sasha was. Nobody had seen her. And Mattie was starting to feel like Sasha didn't want to be found.

The end-of-summer sunshine made every green leaf shimmer and glow like sequins, and the air smelled of pine needles and burnt marshmallows from the night before. It was the kind of day where nothing was supposed to go wrong. But when Mattie realized that her best friend was serious about ditching her, the sun felt too bright, and all those good smells added up to one big stink. She didn't want to keep looking for Sasha.

Even if she was pretty sure where Sasha was.

Beanie acted like Sasha disappearing was no big deal, and maybe it wasn't to Beanie. Your big sister is supposed to want to leave you in the dust every once in a while. But best friends aren't, especially not in the middle of a mystery. Mattie kicked at the dirt with her sneaker.

"Get your clipboard, Beanie. We're doing this without her."

Mattie told Beanie it was her job to write down the license number of any white trucks. But that was mostly so Beanie could keep busy. Really, Mattie was out on the lookout for suspicious people.

As they snaked up and down the campground's twisty lanes, Mattie wondered if she would recognize the two gloopers during the day. The first people she saw who came anywhere close were a tall mom and a shortish dad with two noisy boys packing up their camper van. Mattie took sneaky pictures of those possible gloopers on the old cracked phone, but it ran out of batteries right afterward.

She wrote down the family's license number and the campground slot in her little notebook, noting their descriptions carefully. What were they wearing? How tall did they look? How did they walk?

Beanie didn't seem to notice what Mattie was up to.

She was too focused on *her* job. She hadn't found a single vehicle that matched the description yet, but she kept spinning and looking backward and checking around the trees in case she'd spot one.

Farther down the campground lanes, Mattie noticed a really skinny guy reading an old paperback book in a hammock down by the river. In the right clothes, he could have been the taller glooper. But the pudgy mom and almost grown-up teenage son having a splash fight seemed like a better fit. Mattie added them too.

All the suspects she put in her notebook were the right size and shape, but there was something about the way she remembered the gloopers moving that just didn't fit anyone at the campground. Then, at the end of the loop, Beanie spotted a white truck.

"Aha!" she squeaked, pointing. "It's the truck."

Mattie smiled. It *was* a truck. And it *was* the right color. But it was parked right in front of the Little family cabin. And nobody had driven it anywhere in about fifty years because it didn't have an engine. Or tires.

"Beanie, that's your *dad's* truck."

"I knew he was acting suspicious," Beanie said with her hands on her sides, her elbows jutting out like pokey triangles. "Put him on the list. He's a suspect now."

Mattie couldn't tell if Beanie thought the whole investigation was a game. Mr. Little called the old Ford a classic, and Mrs. Little called it junk, but no way could Mattie call it the gloop truck. Still, she played along with Beanie as she eyed a group of teenagers down at the basketball courts.

"Beanie, write down the license number. I guess we can't rule him out."

"No way, we can't," Beanie nodded. "Last week Mom said she caught him sneaking ice cream in the middle of the night. He could be up to *anything*." She looked super serious.

Usually goofing around with Beanie was fun, but Mattie felt like they were running out of time. Today was an investigation. It felt important. And all of a sudden, she was getting a little tired of Beanie. Still, with Sasha hiding out, Beanie was all Mattie had, and Mattie didn't want to go it alone.

After Mattie was sure she'd added everyone who

looked even a little bit like a glooper to her notebook, Beanie swiped two bags of Swedish Fish from the kiosk store when her mom wasn't looking, and she and Mattie ran back to the donut shop to stake out the parking lot. The noontime rush would bring a fresh crowd of people, and now they were all suspects.

Mattie slipped inside the trailer to plug in Aunt Molly's old phone, just in case she needed it later. Then they sat in the shade of the cypress trees, watching people park their cars. This time Mattie had Beanie write down the color and name of every car, to keep her occupied.

"Just in case, Beanie," she said. "Any of these suspects could have a white truck at home."

Mattie mumbled the car names to Beanie, who scribbled the words and crossed them out again whenever Mattie saw she'd taken them down wrong. Blue Nissan, black Ford, yellow Audi. Silver BMW, red Mini, pink Cadillac. One Hummer, three Mustangs, and a bazillion motor homes. They made it into a game, and every time they spotted a white car, whether it was a truck or not, they ate a gummy fish.

Mattie took notes on all the people who looked like they might be gloopers.

A couple having an argument walked across the parking lot and slammed the doors of their little electric car. The man was tall and skinny. The woman was shortish and round. The angry way they both moved across the blacktop made the back of Mattie's neck prickle, and the couple's little Chevy Volt meant that they couldn't be from *too* far away. Plus it was white. Maybe they had a white truck too. Or was that the silly kind of thinking she'd used to distract Beanie?

The next person Mattie took notes on was Mrs. Mantooth.

She marched up to the donut shop and blasted past the line of people. Mrs. Mantooth wasn't a good neighbor. Mattie knew that. But she wouldn't dump something where it could get into her well water. Would she?

But maybe all her complaining about the water was a trick. An alibi. Mattie had never tasted anything funny in their water, and she didn't think that any gloop could have seeped down into the well . . . not yet. What if Mrs. Mantooth thought no one would suspect her of dumping in that ditch if she was the first to complain about their water? Maybe that's how she planned to get a new well pump out of Aunt Molly.

It wasn't an idea that made much sense, but nothing about Mrs. Mantooth and that well had ever made sense to Mattie.

When they were halfway through their gummy fish, Beanie perked up and poked Mattie in the side. "That guy," she said, pointing, "is definitely up to something."

A scruffy-looking man was leaning against the old pay phone at the edge of the parking lot. He ate the banana fritters from one of Aunt Molly's Banana Boats as he talked, spooning up the syrupy treats from a pink paper tray. Mattie had already ruled him out. Too short. Not stubby.

"He's just using the phone, Beanie. None of the tourist's cell phones work here. I think it's all the trees or the twisty road or something. No way is he a glooper."

"Ohhhh, I wondered what that thing was," Beanie said. When the man hung up, Beanie wandered over to poke at the pay phone's buttons and pretend to make calls.

The pay phone guy tossed the rest of his Banana Boat into the trash as he passed Mattie. Some of the whipped cream didn't make it in and oozed over the side of the bin. A fly buzzed by. Then ten of them. It was like the day's whole investigation: a sticky mess.

THE JELLY HEART
A HEART-SHAPED YEASTED DONUT, DUSTED WITH CINNAMON SUGAR AND FILLED WITH DEEP-RED CHERRY JELLY. SWEET, TART, AND TANGY!

An hour later, Mattie and Beanie's candy bags were empty. The girls hadn't seen any sign of Sasha, and they'd only spotted two more white trucks. One belonged to the volunteer fire chief, whose favorite donut was a Jelly Heart, which just didn't seem like a suspicious kind of donut to Mattie. The other truck belonged to the hermit woman who never talked to anybody.

"Look," whispered Mattie, poking Beanie, who was sprawled in the dirt, staring at clouds.

Beanie popped up and watched Hermit Harriet slam her truck door and lurch across the parking lot. She was about the right size, Mattie thought. Tall and stooped. She could have been the taller person from the night before. But what would Harriet have dumped? She was a carpenter, and that slimy stuff wasn't sawdust.

Harriet usually wore a beat-up pair of jeans and a short-sleeved man's shirt. She kept her long hair in a gray bun that was twisted so tight it looked like a hand grenade. She didn't smile or pass the time with anyone, and whenever she came into the donut shop, all she got was a cup of black coffee.

Never a donut.

Which Mattie *did* find pretty suspicious.

"Do you think it was her?" Beanie shout-whispered.

Mattie watched Hermit Harriet disappear into the shop.

"Maybe," she said, writing down Harriet's license plate.

She was definitely the most likely suspect. Besides being tall, Harriet was grouchy and she drove a white truck with toolboxes in it. Mattie had never seen Harriet Hargrave hanging around a stumpy sidekick, but she'd never seen Harriet with anyone period. The new suspicions made Mattie feel queasy. Even though she'd decided the gloopers might be locals, she still didn't want them to be anyone she knew. In fact, she kind of liked watching Harriet order her coffee with as few words as possible. She liked the puzzle of people like that. Or she used to. Now she was starting to feel like she wasn't even safe at home.

"I'm bored," whined Beanie. "Can we go somewhere else now?"

"Fine," Mattie said.

Mattie knew it was time to find Sasha, even if Sasha wasn't ready to be found. Mattie wanted to run the list of suspects by her. Sasha was great at being suspicious. The feeling wouldn't make *her* queasy. Besides, Mattie was tired of keeping Beanie entertained all by herself.

Since they hadn't found Sasha in all her usual places, Mattie pretty much knew where she'd gone.

The Riverside Inn.

"Let's stake out the parking lot downstream, by the inn and the restaurant," Mattie suggested to Beanie.

Mattie convinced her that it would be easier and more fun to slosh their way toward the inn, splashing down the river rather than walking along the highway. It would take a few more minutes, but Mattie didn't want to go near that road again. Not yet. People easing their cars into parking spots at the donut shop was one thing. A place where cars went speeding by at fifty miles an hour—that was another.

After about ten minutes of slipping their way over the green stones of the riverbank and through the cool water, they reached a restaurant, a general store, and a twenty-room hotel with a big long parking lot all around it. Mattie panted as they trudged up the nearest bank and into the lot. The restaurant had a country band playing out on the huge deck and an outdoor barbeque smoking too. The parking lot was almost full for some end of summer festival. But Mattie wasn't looking for suspects anymore. She'd already spotted Sasha sitting on a hay bale at the edge of the deck. Sasha was bopping to the music and sitting next to her other friend.

Christian Castillo.

Christian's parents managed the inn, and he lived in a special set of rooms upstairs that had no numbers on the doors. Sasha glanced over like she could feel Mattie staring and then looked back at the band, wiggling like the music was the best thing she'd ever seen and Mattie was a stranger.

Or invisible.

Christian hadn't done anything wrong, Mattie reminded herself. He'd never been mean to her. In fact, he and his parents had been super nice in the months after Mattie lost her mom. They let her hang out at the hotel restaurant, nibble on cherries and peanuts from the bar, and watch TV on the smooth leather couch in the afternoons anytime Aunt Molly had to take a trip up to Monterey.

A thing Mattie wasn't willing to do anymore.

She'd been sitting on that hotel couch when Aunt Molly came back with Mom's ashes in an urn. Christian never said anything about it. But still, she hated him just a little bit. Mattie wasn't sure if the hating him was because he was Sasha's Big Sur best friend or if he'd seen her cry. Both, probably.

Beanie zoomed over to the hay bale and crammed herself right between Sasha and Christian. Mattie knew she could go sit down on the hay too. There was room. Sort of. Christian even looked over and smiled. Mattie could squeeze herself into the leftover space.

But Mattie didn't want leftover space.

Especially not after being ditched.

Sasha didn't even look like she wanted Mattie to come over. She always had this weird frozen expression on her face when she was around Christian and Mattie at the same time. Like they weren't supposed to both exist. Like Mattie was butting in just by being alive.

So Mattie stood there.

Arms crossed.

Trying not to glare.

Why couldn't Sasha just believe her? Sasha should have been helping, not sitting around and listening to music. Beanie started whispering into Sasha's ear, and something Beanie said made Sasha glare right back at Mattie.

Now what's she got to be grouchy about? Mattie wondered.

She didn't have to wait very long to find out. Sasha marched over, tugging Beanie by the arm. Sasha's skin was all blotchy at the neck, which was never a great sign.

"You think my dad is a suspect? You think *he* would dump that stupid goo into the river?"

"It's gloo . . ."

Sasha didn't let Mattie finish. Didn't let Mattie explain that it was just some silly idea of Beanie's, and *of course* she didn't suspect Mr. Little. "You can't even get into a car and now you have this weird story about an owl."

Beanie looked back and forth between her older sister and Mattie, like she was trying to figure out who to believe.

"Cut it out or we're not friends," Sasha said.

Beanie's eyes went round as soap bubbles.

Mattie turned around, walked for a few steps, and then ran. She stumbled down the riverbank, hurried over slippery moss-covered rocks with her sneakers still on, splashing water everywhere and not caring. She didn't decide where to go. She just went, until her wet shoes slopped across the black asphalt at Owl's. She went straight for the back door of the donut shop and slammed her shoulder into it, wrenching the handle.

The door swung open, banging against the wall of the shop's back room. Aunt Molly was standing with a tray full of freshly arranged Jelly Hearts.

"What in the . . ."

Aunt Molly whirled to look at Mattie. The tray tilted and donuts went flying. Little sugar-dusted donut hearts plopped all around Mattie's feet.

Without looking up, Mattie lifted her soggy sneaker and stomped. She stomped so hard that a Jelly Heart burst and spurt red rockets of filling halfway across the room.

She stomped until *all* the Jelly Hearts were squished, their insides oozing out of the edges.

THE SQUIRREL SPECIAL
A PETITE PEANUT-ENCRUSTED ÉCLAIR FILLED WITH FLUFFY SALTED CARAMEL CREAM

After Aunt Molly had cleaned up all the broken Jelly Hearts, she plunked Mattie on a stool and took her soppy shoes off. Next, she wiped the sticky cherry spurts from the black-and-white tiled floor and thumped the crushed donuts into the trash.

She didn't get mad.

But she did give Mattie that same worried look from the day before. Worried that Mattie wasn't ready to go back to school. Worried that Mattie wasn't ready to ride the bus.

Once Mattie was done feeling queasy and mad and was just feeling embarrassed and guilty, she tried to explain.

"Me and Sasha had a fight."

She knew it wasn't any excuse for the stomped donut mess and that her explanation wasn't every bit of the truth, but Aunt Molly looked relieved.

"What was it about this time?" Aunt Molly asked, almost smiling.

Mattie tried to think of a way to explain without mentioning the owl, the truck, or the gloop. Which was basically impossible. She shrugged and eyed the trash bin full of donuts. Mattie wanted to complain about Sasha not believing her and about Sasha not taking the investigation seriously, but the explanation that came out of her didn't really have anything to do with owls or investigations or being believed.

"She went off to Christian's and just *left* me," Mattie said.

Maybe that's what the fight *was* about.

For Mattie, anyway.

Aunt Molly leaned in and hugged Mattie. She said stuff about how Big Sur was so small that everybody mostly worked these things out. Mattie had fought with Sasha before, and they always made up, so blah-blah-blah. Mattie didn't really listen. She just let herself be hugged while sneaky tears dribbled down her nose and fell one at a time onto Aunt Molly's apron. Mattie was just old enough to know that grown-ups never fix anything with the things they say, so you don't really have to listen.

You just have to let yourself be hugged.

From the back room, Mattie could hear Martín's favorite radio station playing low under the jingle of customers coming and going, and she didn't want to be anywhere else.

Molly made Mattie help out at Owl's for about an

hour. Not as a punishment, just to keep an eye on her. They made a batch of tiny Squirrel Specials: itty-bitty peanut-encrusted éclairs that Aunt Molly sometimes told kids she left out for the neighborhood squirrels (a thing Mattie knew wasn't true). Aunt Molly stuffed the éclairs with fluffy white caramel cream, and Mattie dipped them in icing and crushed peanuts.

Making donuts with Aunt Molly always evened out Mattie's feelings. No matter what they were. The two of them didn't talk much. It was more like dancing to music that wasn't always playing. Mattie did this. Molly did that. Until they had a perfect batch of treats lined up on a tray.

Mattie didn't actually like the little éclairs. The Squirrel Specials had too much going on, too many tastes. She thought the peanuts were too crunchy and the caramel cream was too sweet. But squirrels still clambered around in her mind while she and Aunt Molly worked. And that gave her an idea.

There was only one person who could possibly help her figure out what was going on, and it wasn't exactly a person.

She needed to find that owl.

And she was tired of waiting for it to show up again.

That's where her squirrel thinking came in.

By the time Aunt Molly placed the last Squirrel Special on the tray, Mattie was calm. She promised Molly she felt fine and she was sorry about all the squished donuts and she was going to go play with Beanie. Which was close to the truth.

Mattie picked up her soppy shoes and quick-stepped her way across the hot parking lot to the trailer. She'd nearly made it to the deck steps when Beanie came huffing and puffing up the path from the river. Beanie ran right into Mattie, because she was looking down and mumbling something under her breath like she was practicing for a spelling test.

"Ooof!" Beanie said, bouncing off Mattie's butt. "You made me forget my lines."

Mattie thunked her soggy sneakers onto the bottom deck step. "What lines?" she asked.

"Sasha said to say . . . that she's sorry about what *she* said, but you have to stop investigating Dad and that rid-rid . . ."

"Ridiculous?" Mattie asked.

"Yeah, that *ridiculous* owl. If you want to hang out."

Mattie didn't bother to explain that they never had been investigating Mr. Little. That would just confuse Beanie. "No dice," said Mattie, folding her arms across her shirt.

"What's that mean?"

"No dice means no way. I can't stop investigating. That gloop could be dangerous. It could be bad for the well or the creek or the river or the campsite or the donut shop."

Mattie glanced back toward Owl's, looking for Aunt

Molly's outline through the shiny windows, feeling more worried than ever.

"I can't tell Sasha *no dice*," Beanie complained.

Something inside Mattie was still feeling squished, even after Aunt Molly's hugging and baking. She turned back to Beanie.

"You don't have to tell her," Mattie said. "Just hang around with me instead. I'm going to go talk to that owl. It's the most important part of the investigation. And you get to help."

Beanie's brown eyes went big, and this time there was nobody else to believe, so she for sure believed Mattie. "*I* get to help?"

"Yup."

"Hoot–hoot," said Beanie, bouncing.

A few minutes later, Mattie and Beanie were standing in front of the Little family toolshed. The padlock gleamed in the summer sunlight.

"I don't know," Beanie said, shaking her head.

"Come on. You do it for your dad, so you can for sure do it for me. Remember, he let you hold the rope when I came down last time."

And it was true. Mr. Little had let Beanie belay Mattie when he'd given them all a climbing lesson. That time, the tree was in the middle of the campground and was covered with colorful plastic handholds and ledges. But still, it had happened.

Lessons like that were important to Mr. Little. He also did all the tree trimming around the cabins. He even did it for Aunt Molly when trees near the trailer or the donut shop started to look raggedy or got too close to the power lines. Thinking about squirrels had gotten Mattie thinking about him, because Mrs. Little joked that he must have been a squirrel in another life.

Mr. Little had ropes, carabiners, helmets, clips, and pulleys, plus fancy spikes that he wore on his shoes and a little sling he could sit in that went around the tree. And most of the big trees in the campground already had climbing pins attached. Most importantly, Mr. Little had taught Beanie to tie all the special knots, which was a responsibility Sasha didn't want. Beanie and Sasha would even belay him down sometimes.

If Beanie could belay the tall and lanky Mr. Little, for sure she could give Mattie a hand, even without her dad's help.

"I bet I know where that owl lives," Mattie said. "You know the big redwood at the edge of the donut shop parking lot? The one with that old eagle's nest? I think your dad already put pins in the tree. I just need you to tie the knots and stuff. And hold the rope. And open the shed."

Mattie stared at Beanie.

Beanie stared right back, nibbling on her bottom lip.

Then she turned to the shed, lifted the padlock, and entered the code. Clunk. The padlock fell open, and little Beanie rolled the squeaky door back. Beams of light pierced the dusty darkness, shining up the rows of metal tools. Rakes, shovels, a gas-powered blower, wheelbarrows, boxes of light bulbs, and stacks of scrap lumber—each tool had a space. If Mr. Little had been a squirrel in another life, then his stash of nuts must have been perfectly organized.

"Beanie, let's grab the stuff and lock up."

Beanie piled carefully wound ropes and spiky shoe clips and clanky carabiners into a giant canvas bag. "We're gonna get caught," Beanie said, shoving the bag into Mattie's hands before sliding the creaky shed door closed.

Clink.

She locked it up, and the girls ran back to the donut shop.

The redwood tree stood at the edge of Aunt Molly's lot, about halfway between the trailer and the shop but a little closer to the ocean than both. Someone had built a square wooden platform onto a branch about halfway up the trunk. Mattie couldn't see the old eagle's nest from the ground, but standing on the deck around the trailer, she would sometimes notice a suspicious silhouette. An owlish shape there in the shadows. Only sometimes. It hadn't seemed important before, but it seemed very important now.

The base of the tree was tucked behind a few smaller pines and a load of fluffy ferns. The perfect cover, Mattie thought. She dropped the bag of equipment at the far side of the redwood, then peeked around. She and Beanie would be basically invisible.

"We're not getting caught," Mattie said.

On the ground a few feet from the redwood tree, Mattie found a pile of old gray owl pellets. "Look," she whispered.

Beanie and Mattie both leaned in close. "Gross-gross-gross," said Beanie. "I can see *bones*."

"Owls barf them up," Mattie told her.

Beanie didn't really look that grossed out, and for a second Mattie was glad that Sasha wasn't around. Peeking a little closer, Mattie noticed that some of the owl pellets had little colorful specs peeking through the matted gray fur and bones. Sprinkles! Mostly pink ones.

"See, told you it likes Aunt Molly's strawberry donuts," Mattie said.

Beanie looked so excited she might explode. She hopped and hooted. "Hoot-hoot, hoot-hoot!"

"Shhhhh," Mattie said. "I don't want to scare the owl away."

Beanie gave Mattie a thumbs-up and shoved her head into the canvas tote bag. She lined up the ropes and the tree sling and two helmets and all the clips and spikes. Each piece, one at a time, on the ground, until everything was super organized.

Everybody thought Sasha was the responsible sister, the tidy sister, the organized sister. Mattie knew that wasn't exactly the truth. And it wasn't just that Sasha didn't want the responsibility of tying Mr. Little's climbing knots. Beanie tied them better. And anything Beanie was better at, Sasha pretended not to like.

Mattie tilted her neck up. The little climbing anchors were all there, shining silver against the red bark of the tree. She would only have to climb a few feet at a time, with the help of the skinny sling, before she hooked into another pin. Through the branches of the redwood, Mattie could faintly make out the owl platform.

She took a jiggety breath.

She had to do it.

Mattie thought for a wild second that maybe she should send Beanie up in the tree instead. They'd brought an extra helmet and everything. But Beanie was so little, and the tree was so high. Mattie was bigger, so she had to do it. Besides, Beanie hadn't met the owl before.

That seemed important.

Whatever the owl had tried to tell Mattie last night wasn't enough. She couldn't call the sheriff's department and tell them to look for two of something. Aunt Molly would say she was letting herself get all worked up, and the other grown-ups would probably laugh. But the more Mattie thought about that gloop, the more afraid she was that it could hurt the donut shop somehow.

"Hook me up," Mattie said. And Beanie went to work.

Clink.

Clank.

Tug.

Yank.

Beanie's tiny hands scuttled around like baby squirrels. She put Mattie's butt into the climbing sling and gave it a good smack. Then Beanie clicked the rope into the first climbing pin, which was only a few feet off the ground. She had to stand on her tiptoes to reach it. Then she grabbed the belay rope and gave Mattie another thumbs-up, a super serious one.

Everything was ready.

Mattie put one slightly shaking foot on the tree trunk and wedged in the little spikes of her shoe clip. She leaned against the climbing sling and lifted her other foot off the ground. The spikes rattled, clinkety-clinkety. She shoved those spikes into the soft redwood bark too and let out a long breath.

She was on the tree.

Mattie was six inches off the ground, but she was on the tree.

Just about ninety-nine more feet to go.

It was a little scary, but not the way cars were. She had the open air all around her, and she could be slow and calm and totally in control. Mattie leaned back and took one more step up and then she carefully pulled the tree sling up too. With her arms out wide, it was almost like she was hugging the tree. Its bark was soft and feathery against her cheek.

Clinkety.

Clinkety.

Shimmy.

Mattie made her way up, clipping the belay rope into a new climbing pin every six feet or so. She could feel the resistance of little Beanie on the rope below. It was working! She glanced down at Beanie once, said a tiny swear, and decided never to look down again. She was going way higher than she had on the climbing tree at the campground.

The owl platform got closer and closer as Mattie inched upward. She was sticky with sweat, and little black ants tickled her skin, but she didn't wipe them away.

"Don't look down, just go up. Don't look down, just go up."

Mattie mumbled her way so high up into the tree that she could see the shushing ocean off in the distance. She was at least forty feet above ground. Her heart pounded faster than the waves, but she couldn't help thinking the view was pretty.

Mattie clipped into the last pin and flicked an ant off her cheek. Then she peeked her nose over the edge of the owl platform. She didn't even want to breathe too loud in case she scared that owl away.

"You better be in there," she whispered.

All Mattie could see was a tangled pile of sticks.

She heaved her belly over the edge, trying not to let her metal spikes get too jingly. Otherwise she might scare the owl away before she got to ask anything. Once Mattie's body was pressed against the wooden platform next to the old nest, all the empty space between her and the ground made her heart beat like a drum. She crept closer to the nest and lifted her head over the edge.

The owl was there!

It had its back to her—probably sleeping—and when the wind blew from off the ocean below, the salty air ruffled the feathers along the bird's back.

How do you wake an owl up? she wondered.

"Psst . . ." she said.

The owl shivered, but nothing else happened.

"Hey," she whispered, hoping nobody in the donut shop was looking up and that nobody in the parking lot was listening.

But the owl didn't wake up.

Mattie knew what to do.

She hooted, deep and low, just like an owl.

The owl swiveled its head and popped its golden eyes open.

Mattie was so surprised she went flat on her stomach again.

Just breathe, she thought. Just breathe. This is why you came up.

She lifted her head over the pile of sticks. The owl hopped closer, crumping across its nest.

"Whoo . . ." it said, putting its beak inches from her face. The sound vibrated through Mattie and tickled the inside of her nose, but she didn't flinch backward. She stared straight into those golden eyes.

"Hi . . . I've got some questions."

THE BLUE MOON
A BRIGHT BLUEBERRY-INFUSED CAKE DONUT DUSTED WITH FRESH CINNAMON AND POWDERED SUGAR

Well, this was unexpected. Alfred knew he'd garnered Mattie's attention, but climbing onto his roost was a bit much. He had to give the girl credit for boldness, though. It had been more than a blue moon since a human had invited themself up to his nest.

After a moment of hesitation, Alfred stepped through his tidy tangle of sticks toward a girl who apparently had questions for him.

Well, *ask*, he thought.

The girl still trembled from her climb. "I need to know what the little crooked lines mean. I need to know if those guys are coming back. I need a license number or . . ."

Her voice trailed off.

Alfred could hear her heart thumping loudly through her thin shirt. Wishing, Alfred was certain, for him to open his beak and do something other than hoot.

Absurd.

Alfred clacked his beak impatiently. Fluffed his feathers in a wave that traveled from his ear tufts down to his talons. The first conversation was always so tiresome, he huffed to himself.

"Let me start over," the girl said. "I'm Mattie—Matilda, but nobody calls me that. Can you, um, wiggle your tufty things if you can understand me?"

Alfred obliged with the smallest of feathery flicks. Twitch-twitch-twitch.

The girl smiled.

Her eyes were hazel, Alfred noticed, not simply green as he'd first thought. Almost golden in places, like his own, and flecked with a deep brown. Pretty eyes alone meant next to nothing, Alfred knew, but he liked them anyway.

Mattie dug around in her pocket and pulled out a cracked black rectangle. An image of his message in the flowerbox shone from the glassy surface. "I need to know what this means."

Alfred leaned forward, swiveling his head and adjusting his eyelids. His message had been exceedingly clear.

At least he had thought so.

"There were two gloopers in that truck," Mattie said. "At first I thought that's what the two lines meant. But that'd be silly. I already knew there were two gloopers. We saw them together. Then I thought maybe the lines meant how many times the gloop truck had dumped that stuff . . ."

Alfred clacked his beak, impatient for the girl, Mattie, to stumble toward something useful.

"Then I thought maybe you were telling me to keep a lookout at a special time . . ."

Alfred gave a soft but hopefully encouraging hoot. Finally she'd arrived at a relevant line of thinking. Time had everything to do with it.

The girl's eyes went wide. "So maybe two in the morning? Or maybe in two more nights?"

Alfred hopped. Yes—she'd gotten it! His nest shuddered beneath him, and Alfred saw Mattie grip the edge of the platform.

"Just blink once for yes, okay?" she suggested.

Alfred blinked obligingly, glad to have that simple form of understanding between them. He couldn't help but be intrigued by this brave creature. Still, he was determined to keep her at wing's length. That was always best.

Then Mattie smiled at him.

And Alfred's ear tufts rose to their full frilly height. It was absolutely involuntary. But a smile will bring a smile.

"So . . . I should be ready for that gloop truck in two more nights? On Tuesday? Do they have, like, a schedule?"

Alfred blinked again. Yes. At least by his best determinations. There had been a regular interval between every visit thus far. It was only logical that the interval would once again repeat.

"How many times have they been to the ditch?" Mattie asked. "Just, um, lift your tufty things, and I'll count."

Alfred lifted his feathered crest—once, twice, three times.

"Okay," said Mattie, nodding. "What else? Is there any evidence I don't know about? Any clues? I've got a list of suspects. I could describe them, and you could do the blinky thing for yes and the beak clacky thing for no."

Alfred blinked, eager to hear Mattie's descriptions.

The wooden platform under his nest gave a jerk. One that had most certainly not originated with him. Mattie grabbed at the edge of the platform again. Alfred swiveled his head to see two small hands grasping the planks. A moment later, a blond, helmeted head with pointy ears and shocked blue eyes peeped over as well.

"Sasha!" Mattie shouted, abandoning all sense of decorum.

In a flustered leap, Alfred hopped to the edge of his nest, swooping over Sasha's head and away from his tree. The gust from his wings unsettled her frizzy blond hair. This was not entirely on accident.

Alfred was relieved that the other girl didn't scream or fall. She was too serious for that. But her arrival meant it was time for an exit, and he disappeared silently into the forest.

Not all children were as understanding as Matilda Waters, Alfred thought. He regretted that this was the case. But he had been acquainted with children like that Sasha before, and it wasn't his job to convince her of the truth.

It was Mattie's.

THE BIG SUR SUNSET
A DOUGHY, YEASTED DONUT ICED WITH SHIMMERY ORANGES AND REDS—GLITTERING, GLOWING, GONE!

Mattie hadn't exactly expected to see Sasha fifty feet up a tree. But she collected herself quickly. This was her chance to prove that she was telling the truth.

The puckered look on Sasha's face made Mattie pretty sure that Sasha had only come up all that way to prove she was lying. And when the owl went swooping over Sasha's head, blowing those frizzy bangs aside, Sasha didn't really look all that surprised. Or even impressed. Like owls flew right over her head every day. She still looked mad, though.

So Mattie had her work cut out for her.

"See," Mattie said, pointing after the disappearing owl. "I told you!"

"So what? You found a bird in a tree—big deal. All this proves is that you are completely out of your mind. Who climbs into an owl nest?"

She scooted forward on her knees and then glared at the messy pile of sticks.

Mattie tried to explain about the hooting and the hopping and the blinking way that the owl had answered her questions. She swore by everything holey and sweet that the owl said the truck would be back in two more nights, so they *had* to set up another stakeout.

"Come on, Sasha. This is important. I'm not lying."

Mattie couldn't tell if Sasha was just pretending to be unconvinced or if she was so mad she couldn't change her mind yet.

"Look, Mattie. Even if you *think* you're telling the truth, all that owl did was scratch and hoot. Totally normal owl stuff. I'm not wasting another night of summer on your weird story and I'm not letting you get us in trouble."

Right then, both girls heard the back door of the donut shop clang open. They scrunched themselves down on the platform, trying to hide from whoever was in the parking lot. Mattie snuck a look around the trunk. It was Aunt Molly, on her way to the trailer.

"I told you this would get us in trouble," Sasha hissed.

"Shhhhh . . ."

Mattie watched Aunt Molly cross the parking lot and disappear down the path to the trailer. "She's probably making lunch. If we get down quick, she won't even know we were up here."

Mattie poked her head over the edge of the platform to check on Beanie. Her brain swirled like a drain. Beanie had two ropes slung over her shoulder.

She gave an extra super serious thumbs-up.

"Beanie's ready," Mattie told Sasha. "You go first."

She thought that Sasha might argue with her, because Sasha liked to be the one to tell people what to do. But instead, Sasha eased herself over the edge. The little pulley rasped as she went down, but that was the only sound in the forest. Sasha floated to the ground like a dry sycamore leaf.

When Beanie gave Mattie the next thumbs-up, Mattie tucked Aunt Molly's cracked phone into her pocket. She wished she'd had a chance to tell the owl about her list of suspects, but she was looking down at a different problem.

So far up in the tree, her heart wasn't acting in its normal thumpy-bumpy way. It was acting like a defective wind-up monkey, doing flips and not landing on its feet. Sure, maybe being up in a tree wasn't as scary as being in a speeding car. But it wasn't as cozy as being tucked in a booth at Owl's either, and the open air didn't make her feel so free anymore.

"Come on, Mattie," she whispered to herself, easing her weight onto the rope and hoping Beanie was really ready to lower her.

The owl platform shrank in Mattie's view as she floated downward through the trees. Her stomach filled with the emptiness of falling. The sounds of the highway and the ocean and her thumpy heart swirled together in her ears until . . .

Bump.

She fell onto her butt and let herself flop back onto the prickly needles covering the forest floor. She made it. She'd totally talked to the owl too. Sort of. And without getting into any trouble for climbing without a grown-up. But a second later, she knew they were in a bigger kind of trouble. That owl, just looking into its eyes, made Mattie sure that whatever was going on was important.

She'd been right.

That goo was no good, and the sneaky gloop dumpers would definitely be back.

"Is it my turn now?" Beanie said, hovering over Mattie still flopped onto her back.

"Absolutely *not*," Sasha said, before Mattie could answer.

The girls got everything packed up and back into the locked shed without getting caught. It was kind of a miracle. But once everything was put away, Sasha stomped home. She slammed the cabin door so hard Mattie could feel the sound inside her ears for moments afterward, till it was clear Sasha wasn't coming back out. It had been a while since Sasha was so seriously mad. In fact, if Sasha kept track of how angry she got, she might have set a new record after chasing Mattie up the redwood. But Mattie didn't feel like she had had a choice.

She had needed to get to that owl.

Mattie turned to Beanie. "Two nights."

"Two nights!" Beanie said, holding up two fingers on each hand, which Mattie couldn't help but notice made four. Whatever. Beanie understood.

Aunt Molly must have walked back to the shop by the time Mattie got home. In the quiet of the empty trailer, Mattie marked the night of the next glooping on her calendar with a big black dot. Which made her eyes wander to the gold star on top of the first Tuesday in September. Seven more days until the start of school. That should be plenty of time to be ready to ride the bus, even if Mattie didn't feel that way yet.

First she had to catch those gloopers in the act.

She'd figure out the school bus thing later.

That night, Aunt Molly made vegetable soup in her crockpot, and they ate it with fresh crispy French rolls from the Big Sur Bakery. Mattie slept with her window open and listened for hooting or tapping or squealing tires in case she'd been wrong about the owl's messages. She heard a thump on the deck. Mattie flung her covers off, scampered outside, and came face to face with a super chubby raccoon. She panted, out of breath, while the raccoon sauntered down the steps and disappeared into the ferns.

Two hours after that false alarm, a squeal on the highway made Mattie reach for her window. She flicked her curtains open just in time to see a motor home with a flat tire shimmy onto the edge of Owl's parking lot.

But there was no sign of the gloop truck or the owl.

That meant that the owl was right. Mattie was almost sure of it. The gloopers would be back, but not until Tuesday night. Still, part of Mattie wondered if she'd been wrong about the owl. Wrong to believe that she could really understand his wiggles and hops and hoots. She yawned and fell asleep without meaning to.

On Tuesday morning, Mattie checked the scraggly redwood tree for signs of the owl, but the bird wasn't perched there. There was no owlish shadow in the nest or on the branch above. She'd have felt better if she could at least see a hint of him.

Sasha had calmed down a little. She hadn't disappeared to the Riverside Inn to hang out with Christian again. She wasn't glaring one-hundred-percent of the time either. But she wouldn't even look at Mattie's list of suspects, and she got crossing-her-arms mad all over again when Mattie asked if she was coming over for the stakeout that night.

But Mattie had to ask.

The queasy feeling that gloop gave Mattie wouldn't go away. It could be toxic. It could get all the way down to the beaches or seep deep into the ground and into their well. No way could Aunt Molly afford to drill a new one that would keep the gloop out—she couldn't even afford a new pump. Plus, Mattie wasn't sure what the gloop would do to all the animals.

The turkeys and jays and banana slugs.

The sea otters and frogs and fish.

The owl.

If she could just prove that the white truck was up to something dangerous, she knew Sasha would understand. Sasha cared about the creek and the river and the campground and the donut shop just as much as Mattie. It was one of the reasons they were friends. Mattie held on to the hope that whatever she found on the second stakeout would fix things between them. By the time school started, Sasha wouldn't be mad, and the donut shop and the campground would be safe. There were six days left. Which felt like plenty of time to prove to her best friend that she wasn't a liar or losing her mind.

That Tuesday took forever.

It oozed like a slug across a rock. Barely moving, but then . . . it was gone. Disappeared into the ferns and redwoods. When Beanie banged on the door that evening, Mattie hopped up and headed to the deck without asking if Sasha was coming.

She knew Sasha wasn't.

When Sasha Little was crossing-her-arms mad, she did not change her mind.

Mattie sighed and watched the sun sink into the Pacific Ocean. Beanie fidgeted next to Mattie outside the trailer, trying to get a jay to eat a peanut out of her hand, but she was never still enough. When Beanie got frustrated, Mattie handed over Aunt Molly's cracked phone, telling her to plug it in and play a game, hoping she'd keep herself busy that way.

Mattie checked again for the outline of the owl in the evening shadows. It hadn't come back.

The sky beyond the owl's perch in the redwood glowed orange and pink like one of Aunt Molly's sunset donuts, but it didn't feel pretty or peaceful.

Not to Mattie.

THE SPRINKLE EMERGENCY
A CLASSIC GLAZED CRULLER ENCRUSTED WITH JEWEL-TONED SANDING SUGAR STRIPES

Alfred had positioned himself in a pine tree near Mattie's trailer with an optimal view of the highway. He stared up the winding road, and the golden reflectors studding it shone through the drifting fog like scales of a giant snake. His wings began to twitch as the first glimmer of headlights alerted him to the approaching vehicle half a mile up Highway One.

An insistent mosquito buzzed at the edge of his vision, but he did not swivel his head to glare at it. Then something below him let out a soft grumble.

The girl with the frizzy blond hair. Sasha.

What was she doing out of bed?

He twitched his ear tufts. The girl was quietly complaining about another night of summer wasted on Mattie's owl obsession. About how *nothing* was going to happen. Alfred clacked his beak at that.

Something *was* happening, and she was about to be in the way!

The big white truck crept around the bend. Squeaky and slow. The truck's headlights flicked off before it pulled to the side of the road, but the glow of its red brakes stained the night fog pink.

As Alfred peered down, he saw Sasha sneak across the highway and hide herself behind a clump of rocks. In her hands she held a small box. One of those things that tourists carried around to point at children or slugs, shouting *cheese* and making strange snapping sounds. Alfred scoffed. That silly little thing wouldn't work in the dark.

Sasha leaned over the rocks, pointing the camera at the truck.

Zip-zip-zip click!

Alfred flinched at the noise.

The two shadowed figures slunk out of the truck, and Sasha moved the camera along with them from behind her hiding spot. Zip-zip-zip click!

Alfred stretched his wings nervously, hoping the dumpers wouldn't hear the noisy little camera over their banging doors.

Where was the hazel-eyed girl? Where was Mattie?

What a terrible muddle!

And just when he thought of her, Mattie appeared. Alfred hadn't heard the trailer door fling open in all the kerfuffle. Seeing her barefoot in the donut shop parking lot squeezed at his nerves. She ran gingerly across the gravel, rushing toward trouble.

Mattie's skin prickled against the cold under her mom's old T-shirt. She darted along the edge of the parking lot, prancing over pebbles in her bare feet. She had snatched Aunt Molly's old phone out of a sleeping Beanie's hand before running out into the night.

That owl was right.

Those gloopers were back!

Mattie hid behind a tree trunk at the edge of the Owl's parking lot. She lifted the phone and jabbed the button below the screen, impatient to get to the camera. The screen went white and then flashed a tiny empty-battery icon back at her. She pushed the button again, not wanting to believe it. But the phone was dead.

A flash burst from a clump of boulders on the opposite side of the road, lighting up the reflectors along the highway. The sudden dazzle of light gave Mattie a look at the gloopers' clothes, but it also sent the pair of them scrambling toward the back of the truck.

Hovering near the truck's bumper, the gloopers glared over at the boulders where the flash had lit everything up. But rather than investigate, they began to shove at each other, flinging the hose around. Before Mattie had moved another five steps, the truck was squealing around the corner.

They were gone.

Mattie kicked a pinecone with her bare foot. Which is always a big mistake. Hopping along with a bleeding big toe, Mattie wasn't sure what she would find. Everything had happened so quickly, she hadn't even paid attention to the truck's license plate.

"So stupid," she said, hopping a little slower.

But sore toe or not, there was a new mystery to investigate. What was that flash?

When Mattie got a couple feet from the highway, she stopped, staring down at the asphalt. Her heart hammered as she listened for the hiss of a coming car. She looked both ways, checking for headlights, and limped across the road.

Peering into the ditch, Mattie saw the shine of a new puddle of slime. It shimmered all the way down to the pipe that went under the highway. She didn't think those dumpers had had time to unload a whole batch of whatever it was, but the ugly goopyness of it made Mattie feel hopeless.

That's when the sirens echoed down the road.

Mattie teetered at the edge of the ditch as the flashing lights and blazing high beams of a cruiser blinded her. She stumbled and fell back down the ditch, out of the car's path but scrambling to keep herself out of the gloop.

Gravel crunched. A door slammed. The car's siren clicked off. Blue and red lights bounced off the tree trunks above her. A flashlight's bright glare swung through the branches before sliding over the rim of the ditch and lighting her up.

Mattie, in her pajamas, with a bleeding toe, next to a trail of sour slime.

She blinked up into the light. The cruiser had slowed to a stop, but she felt like it was still speeding right at her. Mattie knew she must have looked suspicious, but she also knew she had about thirty seconds to convince the flashlight shiner to chase down that gloop truck. They were getting away!

"Miss?" The voice and outline of the man behind the light were husky and tough.

Mattie took a breath so big it was like swimming in the ocean. "They went that way," Mattie pointed. "In a big white truck with a hose on the back. You've got to go get them."

"Miss, please walk up the embankment."

She limped up the side of the ditch. Once the man stopped shining his flashlight into her face, Mattie could see that he was from the sheriff's office. The gold star on the side of his car gleamed in the fog.

There was a deputy already writing something down in her very official looking notebook. Great. The other deputy, the one who had stepped outside the cruiser, reached out and put his hand on Mattie's elbow.

Very gently.

When he touched her, Mattie noticed that she was shivery shaking.

"Let's get you home," he said.

Mattie knew the deputy's name without even

checking his badge. She remembered his voice. He was the same one who drove down the highway from Monterey to tell them about Mom.

She let Deputy Nuñez tug her across the road.

Crossing the highway was easier with him holding on to her arm. Deputy Nuñez had always been nice. More than that, he'd always been honest. Mattie knew he was a person she could trust. But walking beside him made the night harder too. He reminded her of the things she couldn't fix. Couldn't save. Couldn't have again.

As they stepped back onto the donut shop parking lot, tears plunked onto her shirt.

How could she explain the white truck without everybody thinking she'd invented some horrible story to . . . to what? She couldn't guess why a grown-up would think she had made up her story, but they would have a reason. Deciding why she'd lied would be easier than believing her.

When Mattie looked up, Aunt Molly was on the deck outside the trailer in her pajamas. She looked a little worried, but not confused. She looked like she'd been expecting something like this to happen.

Deputy Nuñez's partner pulled the county car into the parking spot just in front of Owl's. She eased out of the cruiser, shut the door, and waited on the concrete sidewalk while Deputy Nuñez walked Mattie home.

His shiny black shoes crunched against the pine needles that poked against Mattie's bare feet. He stopped at the end of the path, before the start of the deck steps, and didn't let go of Mattie's arm.

"Hi, Ms. Waters," Deputy Nuñez said. "We'll need to get a statement."

Aunt Molly nodded and tried to smile. "Okay. We've got one of Mattie's friends asleep inside. Let's go over to the shop and have some coffee."

"Couldn't hurt," said Deputy Nuñez.

Aunt Molly quietly closed the trailer door and swept down the stairs like she wasn't embarrassed to be wearing her pajamas and talking to a sheriff's deputy in the middle of the night. Deputy Nuñez finally let go of Mattie's elbow, and Aunt Molly wrapped an arm around her. All Mattie wanted to do was be crumpled into a big hug. But that would have to wait. She shuffled through the pile of clues in her brain. Tried to think of what else she could have done. How else she could have busted those gloopers.

She'd messed everything up.

She had zero proof to show Deputy Nuñez.

She got caught out in the ditch at midnight.

And no way was that truck coming back now.

Whatever trouble was on the way because of that gloop, Aunt Molly would have to fix it. And Mattie didn't know if she could.

Deputy Nuñez's partner hadn't turned off the cruiser lights, and they bounced all over the place as Aunt Molly unlocked the shop's front door. They were brighter than a donut covered in shiny red sugar.

Too bright.

Molly insisted on making both deputies fresh cups of coffee. Mattie slipped into her favorite booth and stared at the tabletop. Deputy Nuñez took a sip and started in on the questions. "So, Miss Mattie, what were you doing out on the highway in the middle of the night? Are you the one who called 9-1-1?"

Mattie crinkled her eyebrows, confused. "There was this truck . . . it's been dumping stuff," Mattie faltered. Aunt Molly looked at Deputy Nuñez.

"I wanted to catch them in the act, so I took Aunt Molly's old phone to get a picture, but Beanie must have unplugged it even though I told her not to. And they . . . they got away. But *I* didn't call 9-1-1."

Deputy Nuñez sighed and nodded. His partner stopped writing in that awful black notepad. Aunt Molly rubbed her shoulder. Mattie knew what they would all say. Exactly what Sasha said.

That Mattie had made the truck up and then had got so scared she called 9-1-1. They'd say owls don't talk and flowerpots don't fly.

Would they even check the gloop out? Mattie shivered in her pajama shirt. In her mom's pajama shirt.

She couldn't say anything else.

They wouldn't believe her.

"I think you should get her back to bed, Ms. Waters. We'll check in tomorrow and get that statement."

The deputies said goodnight and backed out of the parking spot. After giving Mattie a look that said I love you anyway, Aunt Molly slipped into the back to put the empty coffee cups into the washer and clean up.

Then the front door slid open.

So softly the bells didn't jingle.

Sasha snuck into the shop. She put her finger to her lips, like her being there was a secret. Which, Mattie guessed it was. But at least Sasha wasn't the one who had been caught out on the highway in the middle of the night. Mattie didn't have the energy to keep fighting everybody.

"I messed it all up," she whispered. "I didn't get any proof, and now they think I'm the one who was up to something."

"You didn't mess up," Sasha whispered back, pulling a crushed wind-up camera from her pocket. "*I* did, because I didn't believe you."

The wind-up camera's domed lens was cracked down the middle. "I only turned the flash on for the last picture, because I thought they'd notice. They definitely did. Then, when I was running away, I fell, and the camera got kind of crunched. But I saw it."

Mattie's mouth dropped open. She didn't even bother to swipe her tears away. "The gloop truck?" she asked.

"Yep," said Sasha, nodding. "I called the police from the pay phone in the parking lot as soon as I saw that truck pull over."

"That was *you*?"

"Yeah," Sasha said. "It's almost a good thing we get such bad reception around here. If I'd called from my dad's cell phone, I bet the deputies would be headed to my house next."

Sasha looked down at the table instead of at Mattie. "I didn't mean for you to get in trouble. Sorry. But don't worry. We'll figure something out." She looked back up and gave Mattie a little scrunched smile.

Mattie's thinking swirled like ice cream and hot fudge. The owl. The truck. The gloop. Sasha believed her and Sasha was sorry. Mattie could tell.

The sound of Aunt Molly clanging in the back room made Sasha flinch.

"Come to my house in the morning," Sasha whispered, stuffing the camera back into her pocket. With that, she zipped out the door and ran across the parking lot.

Aunt Molly poked her head out of the back room. "Did the deputies come back? I thought I heard the door."

"Nope," Mattie said, sitting up straighter. "Just your imagination."

She let herself be hugged, but inside the hug, her mind stopped swirling until all she could see was that gloop. Shiny, wet, stinky gloop.

Gloop that even Sasha knew was big trouble.

THE S'MORE BOMB
A ROUND, YEASTED DONUT FILLED WITH PUFFY MARSHMALLOW CREAM AND TOPPED WITH A HAZELNUT-MILK-CHOCOLATE GLAZE AND GRAHAM CRACKER CRUNCHIES!

The next morning, Mattie pushed herself up in bed and saw Aunt Molly outside on the deck, staring across the highway at some bright yellow caution tape. It was blocking off the ditch. That meant the sheriff's deputies coming last night hadn't been all bad. The deputies must have noticed the gloop. And now maybe Aunt Molly knew that the gloop could be trouble too. But somehow that didn't make Mattie feel any better. She knew now that grown-ups weren't always able to fix things. Even when they wanted to. Even when they tried.

Aunt Molly was going to need her help.

Mattie crawled across a still-snoring Beanie and tiptoed out onto the deck. She hugged her goose-bumpy arms in the morning chill. Next to her, Aunt Molly sighed and put her mug of tea down on the rail.

Steam curled up into the air.

"Does Mrs. Mantooth know yet?" Mattie asked.

Aunt Molly flattened her mouth into an I'm-trying-not-to-worry line and pulled Mattie in for a sideways hug. "Don't worry about that, kiddo. I'm sure this will all be fine. I'm sorry those dumpers have been waking you up in the middle of the night, but the officers will figure out what's been going on. Your job is to have the best last six days of summer ever."

A little *less* than six days, Mattie thought. Aunt Molly was counting today too, which wasn't something Mattie ever did. To Aunt Molly, a dozen donuts was always thirteen. But although it was still morning, Wednesday had already slipped by a little bit. So there were really only five days of summer left. But Mattie didn't correct her aunt. And she didn't argue with Molly about the sheriff's department being able to figure out what was going on.

Even if, last time, they never were.

Just then, Mrs. Mantooth came mincing down her driveway and across the parking lot. Her black leggings and fleece sweater were crisp and sharp in the fuzzy morning light. Even though she was on the official suspects list in Mattie's notebook, Mattie didn't really think that she was a glooper. She'd decided nobody would dump bad stuff near their own well. Not even Mrs. Mantooth. Besides, she was enough trouble as a neighbor already.

"Mattie, why don't you take Beanie home and play at the Little's for a while?" Aunt Molly asked. "I need to go talk with Mrs. Mantooth. Have fun—no worrying—okay?"

She turned toward the deck steps but waited for Mattie to answer.

"Okay," Mattie said, hoping it wasn't a lie. She'd try not to worry. But she had to catch the gloopers before Mrs. Mantooth could make too much of a fuss. She'd make sure Aunt Molly's donut shop was safe. And she wasn't going to count on the county sheriff.

Not again.

Aunt Molly swept down the deck steps, off to intercept Mrs. Mantooth before she could make it to their trailer. She had left her tea steaming on the railing, and the scent of peppermint prickled in Mattie's nose.

Mattie hurried inside and changed into her softest T-shirt, her shorts with the biggest pockets, and a fuzzy green fleece with even more pockets. She loaded the pockets up with Aunt Molly's old phone, a charger, and her notebook. She almost put the jar of gloop into her jacket pocket too, but she'd already showed that to Sasha. Besides, it might break.

Before leaving, she shook Beanie awake. "Come on, we've got to get Sasha—I'll explain on the way."

Beanie blinked a couple times and hopped out of bed. She had to hike her pajama bottoms up by the time they got to the creek. But she splashed along behind Mattie, nodding while Mattie tried to explain about the stakeout and the deputies and Sasha.

Over at the Little Family Campground, Sasha was already awake. As soon as Mattie made it up the bank and into the campground, she heard Sasha's window rattle open. Sasha knelt in her top bunk, peering down, waiting for them to arrive.

"Beans, grab some cereal from the kitchen," she said through the opening. "We need to have a meeting." Then she rattled the window closed again.

Beanie looked up at Mattie.

"Told you she believes us," Mattie said.

"How'd you do that?" Beanie asked with amazement.

"I didn't. She figured it out by herself."

Beanie huffed up the back stairs and charged into the kitchen. Somehow she got two boxes of cereal, a carton of milk, and three bowls and spoons to fit within her tiny arms. She was like an octopus. Mattie kind of wished she had snuck over some of Aunt Molly's Wednesday specials. The S'more Bomb was a serious donut for serious thinking.

But cereal would have to do.

Sasha thumped to the floor in one jump when Beanie and Mattie came in with breakfast. She snatched a box of granola from Beanie, crammed her hand in, and crunched away.

"All right," she said. "Let's list what we know about these . . ."

"Gloopers?" Mattie suggested.

"Right. Gloopers it is."

Mattie pulled her notebook out of her pocket, happy to finally have Sasha on her side. "Let's start with the night of the broken pot. The owl tapped on my window and woke me up, spinning its head toward the road three times so I'd notice the white truck. I saw *two* people. One skinny and tall. One shorter, but not *short*-short, and roundish. That one was wearing a hooded sweatshirt. They were both doing something with a floppy hose when the owl dropped or threw or maybe pushed a flowerpot off the trailer."

"Let's stick to the facts," Sasha interrupted, making a face. "A pot got smashed. You didn't actually see the owl do it, right?"

Mattie squeezed the little notebook. Working with Sasha was never going to be one-hundred-percent easy.

"What happened next?" Sasha said, trying to ignore the whole owl thing.

Mattie sucked in a breath. At least she had Sasha listening. "The gloopers heard the crash and sped off. I didn't get their license plate, and Aunt Molly woke up."

"Okay, next!" Sasha said, pacing.

"The gloop clue. It came the day after. The owl visited me at the campground—I'm sure it was following me around until I was alone—and it dropped a load of gravely gloop for me to find."

Mattie raised her eyebrows, waiting for Sasha to question her account of the owl, but this time Sasha didn't interrupt.

"That's when we became detectives!" Beanie said, raising her spoon.

"Right," Mattie replied. "The gloop trail. We found more stinky goo at the side of the highway, right where that truck had been parked the night before. It looked like people had dumped the gloop a few times. Some of it was almost dried up."

Sasha squished her mouth like she wanted to hurry past the part of the story where she'd been so totally wrong, so Mattie charged ahead.

"Night two," she said. "The owl woke me up and left the second clue. Two jiggety lines drawn in the flowerbed with its talon."

Now Sasha couldn't help interrupting. "Come on, Matt. How do you know it was some special message? It didn't look like anything to me."

Mattie was determined not to get off track. She didn't have time to try to convince Sasha of something Sasha didn't already believe, because that would take forever. She flipped to the next page in her notebook. "Focus, Sasha. I still need to show you the list of suspects I made."

"We made," Beanie squeaked.

Mattie nodded at Beanie.

Sasha stopped pacing and peeked over Mattie's shoulder to read the descriptions. She poked at the list of people from the campground. "That guy checked out this morning. The mom and her teenage son are still here . . . Those guys are gone."

Sasha narrowed her eyes when she got to the notes about Mrs. Mantooth, the angry arguing couple, and Hermit Harriet from the donut shop parking lot. "Why don't you have that Mr. Slug guy on the list? I saw him drive by yesterday."

Mattie shook her head. "No, Mr. Slug only comes on Sundays. Besides, he's an old friend of my grandma's. You must have seen somebody else."

Sasha shrugged. "Well, I would make *her* suspect number one," she said, pointing to Mrs. Mantooth's name.

"But . . ." Mattie stumbled, trying to explain why that couldn't be. Mrs. Mantooth's demands about the well had her worried, but she didn't really think Mantooth was a glooper.

Sasha crunched on another handful of granola. "And Hermit Harriet should be number two. She's definitely suspicious. There's a trail that goes right behind her old shed. We should go snoop around."

Mattie wasn't so sure.

She felt like they were still missing something.

Her mind ticked through all the customers who'd come into Owl's over the last few weeks. Lines and lines of people. Tourists, regulars, friends, neighbors. All the happy parents and kissy couples, the silly slug man, and old wrinkled grandparents driving swanky new motor homes. There were too many people to consider. They had to find some clue that narrowed it down.

Something from the night before *had* to point them in the right direction.

Mattie flipped to her next page of notes.

"Last night. When the truck pulled up, I grabbed the old phone and ran outside. But it was dead." Mattie paused to shoot Beanie a look. "And then Sasha's flash went off. I didn't get the license number, again, because they drove off so fast."

"Sorry," Beanie said through a mouthful of cereal. "I didn't mean to forget to plug it in. Besides, the stakeout was boring without Sasha."

Mattie wasn't mad. Well, she was a little bit mad about the phone, but she wasn't mad about Beanie saying a sleepover was boring without Sasha.

It kind of was.

Mattie raised her eyebrows, wishing Sasha would say sorry too, but she didn't. The flash from the disposable camera had scared the gloopers away, keeping Mattie from getting the license plate number. But it could also be their best hope of finding out who dumped the gloop.

"So, did you get a picture?" Mattie asked Sasha. "Was that flash worth it?"

Mattie had been wondering about the camera all morning. The flash had come from the boulders across the highway. If Sasha had been even halfway pointing the camera in the right direction—which, knowing Sasha, she absolutely was—then she would have to have a good picture of the gloopers. Maybe even their license plate.

"I snapped *three* pictures on the click camera," Sasha said, finally sitting down. "Two before the one with the flash. But we can't see them yet."

She slid her hand into her pocket and pulled out the green and black click camera. The girls passed it around their little circle.

"Busted," said Beanie.

"It's so light," Mattie said, lifting it up. It didn't look promising, that smashed-up cardboard-and-plastic box. "Do you think it'll still work?"

"Course it will," Sasha said. But then she didn't look so sure. "I mean . . . it got cracked *after* I took the pictures, so I bet they're totally fine."

She grabbed the camera back and stuffed it into her pocket.

Mattie knew Sasha didn't want to admit that maybe there was no good picture on that camera. Mattie didn't want to think it either. But they both knew it was a possibility.

"We just have to get the pictures *developed*," Sasha said. "If I got a good picture, which I bet I did, then we can show it to that deputy guy. But let's see the photos before telling anybody else. I'm not getting into trouble for sneaking out onto the highway if the pictures are all blurry and black. We can take the camera somewhere special, and they'll print the pictures out on shiny paper just like in the olden days."

This is when Mattie got nervous.

Really nervous.

Her head started to feel like a soda on a summer day. Fizzy. Bubbly. Warm. She knew that there was nowhere in Big Sur to get photos developed. There wasn't even a big grocery store or a pharmacy. You had to go to Carmel or Monterey for stuff like that. You had to ride in a car or a bus for stuff like that.

Which was definitely going to be a problem.

One that Mattie couldn't ignore.

Not anymore.

THE BIRTHDAY BAR
OUR BIGGEST YEASTED DONUT BAR, ICED WITH CHOCOLATE
AND EXPLODING WITH SPRINKLES. EVERY BIRTHDAY BAR
COMES WITH A SPARKLER CANDLE. FIZZ-WIZZ-POP!

Once Mattie understood Sasha's plan to get those pictures developed, she started to ramble. Hoping she could keep Sasha from saying what she was already thinking.

"I . . . I could ask the owl what we should do next," Mattie suggested.

"No way. You're not climbing that giant tree again. If the owl wants you to know something, it can fly down. *We* have to do something now. It's our turn, Matt."

Mattie squeezed her notebook, squishing the metal spirals into her palm.

"Come here," Sasha said, grabbing a scrap of paper from a messy nightstand piled with books and half-finished water glasses. She held the slip of paper up like a tiny flag. "Dad said you can get pictures developed in like an hour at a drugstore. But I figured we should call this place just to be sure. It's where my mom gets Beanie's inhalers. I copied the number down from the prescription box."

Mattie followed her into the kitchen. Beanie bumped along behind them. Sasha picked up the receiver of the ancient white telephone the Littles kept on their kitchen counter. She punched buttons, checking numbers on the scrap of paper every few punches.

Sasha waited while the phone rang, and then Mattie could hear the echoing of a voice recording. Sasha frowned and punched another number.

"Hi," Sasha said, leaning closer so Mattie could hear. "We wanted to know if you still develop pictures. Like from a disposable camera?"

Mattie heard the answer float through the air. *Yep, in the photo department. It's $12.99 for a roll of twenty-four pictures.*

Beanie climbed onto the kitchen counter, squishing her head up to the receiver so she could hear too.

"Cut it out," Sasha whispered, pushing her off the counter.

Beanie bumped her head on a cabinet on the way down. She rubbed at her forehead once her feet were firmly on the kitchen floor. That's when Mrs. Little walked up the back steps onto the porch, her arms full of groceries.

"Mom, Sasha hit me!" Beanie yelled through the screen door, still rubbing her forehead.

When Mrs. Little came through the door, Sasha already had her hands up in the air. "I did *not* hit Beanie," she said.

"She didn't Mrs. Little," Mattie said. "Honest."

Mrs. Little sighed and gave Sasha *the look* before setting down her grocery bags.

"Sorry, Mom," Sasha said. "Come on, Beanie—let's go play in our room."

The girls escaped down the hall, and Sasha closed the door behind them.

"See?" she said. "I told you. They can develop the pictures, but we have to go there. It's up in—"

"Monterey," said Mattie.

"Yeah," Sasha said. "And we'd have to take a—"

"Bus," said Mattie.

"And the only one who's ever taken the bus up to Monterey is—"

Mattie didn't say anything.

"Who?" Beanie asked, boinging up onto her knees, forgetting about her banged forehead.

Sasha sighed. "Come on, Mattie. We'll never get permission if you don't go with us. No way is our mom saying yes if it's just me and Beanie. But she trusts you. You know the trip. You did it a hundred times last summer. I know you're not a chicken, Matt!"

Mattie stared at the dry scabs on Sasha's knees.

Her breathing got faster.

Sasha was right. Mattie knew the bus route and she *had* done it about a hundred times. Every school break, starting when Mattie was eight, if Mattie's mom couldn't find a few days off from her law office, she would send

Mattie down to Big Sur on the bus. Aunt Molly always met her at the stop by the campground. Mattie would stay a week, have fun with Sasha and Beanie, stuff herself with donuts, and then Aunt Molly would send her back up to Monterey on the same bus.

A trip up the highway used to feel easy.

Fun, even.

Super grown-up and responsible.

She'd ride up front right behind the driver, Janelle, and they would play Jell-O together on the twisty roads. Miss Janelle would even let her pick the radio station sometimes.

The last time Mattie rode that bus, Janelle dropped her off like always. Aunt Molly met her out on the highway, and Mattie played with Sasha and Beanie all spring break. Then Mom decided to come down for the weekend. She left Monterey after work. Mattie wasn't with Mom then, so she only knew a few things about what happened next.

She knew it was raining.

She knew there was a big dark truck.

She knew that it crossed the double yellow line, running her mom's car off the road, and just drove away.

People said the accident wasn't her mom's fault. Mattie agreed with that.

It was hers. If she'd stayed at home for spring break, it wouldn't have happened. If she'd taken the bus back, it wouldn't have happened.

She'd been scared ever since. Hadn't ridden in a single vehicle. But not getting into a car or a bus wasn't just about being afraid. It wasn't just about going too fast, swerving around corners, and maybe getting crunched.

It was more than that.

It had probably always been more than that.

She wanted to stay safe, sure, but she also wanted to stay put. Staying in Big Sur, she could feel like she wasn't getting any older. It could still be spring break, and she could still believe that Mom was coming back to get her.

Mattie used to know what was waiting for her on the other side of a trip. Donuts with Aunt Molly or being home with Mom. Good snuggly things. Now the end of every possible trip seemed fuzzier. Darker. Dangerous. If she rode up to Monterey, she'd arrive in the place that used to be home, but her mom wouldn't be waiting there when she did. Mattie knew it didn't all make sense, but that didn't mean it wasn't real.

The feeling.

Even the idea of shorter rides made her nervous. She thought she'd be using the last days of summer to get ready to take the school bus. To *feel* ready. But she was starting to think that might never happen. The trip to school wasn't going to be any different than a trip to Monterey. She'd have to start something new, and Mom wouldn't be there.

She didn't want that to feel real.

Not yet.

"I can't do it, Sasha," she said, trying not to cry. "We have to think of something else." She squeezed at her notebook until her hand hurt and looked anywhere but at Sasha and Beanie.

Sasha didn't get mad. She even gave Beanie a shut-up look when it seemed like Beanie was going to ask another question. But she also crossed her arms and waited, nibbling on her lip. Like she knew they weren't about to think of any other plan.

Staring at Sasha's sureness make Mattie feel hot and prickly sweaty.

"Let's go look for the owl," Mattie said, heading down the hall. "Maybe . . . maybe it knows something else. Something important. I can ask."

Sasha didn't bother to say no again. She nudged Beanie, and they followed Mattie toward the door. The sisters whispered a little behind her, but all Mattie heard was Sasha hissing, "Just wait, Beans."

When the three girls got to the parking lot outside Owl's Outstanding Donuts, the deputies' cruiser was back. Plus another official looking car that said Environmental Services Agency on the side. The ditch across the road was still roped off with bright yellow caution tape. And there was a red sheet of paper posted in the window of the donut shop.

It said, *NOTICE OF CLOSURE*, and then a bunch of stuff in tiny print that Mattie didn't really understand.

Mattie tugged at the shop's front door. It was locked.

Inside, Aunt Molly was sitting at a booth with Deputy Nuñez, his partner, and some stranger. When Molly saw the girls, she rushed to the door to let them in.

If the bell jingled, Mattie didn't hear it.

"Beanie, I'm sorry, but I can't make you your Birthday Bar," Aunt Molly said.

"What?" Beanie asked, all confused.

"It's your birthday," Sasha reminded her. "Didn't Mom tell you?"

"Oh yeah," Beanie said.

"Come on in, girls," Aunt Molly said, waving them toward a booth. "I had to shut down the kitchen. Just temporarily."

Aunt Molly signed a bunch of papers, and the deputies and the woman from the Environmental Services Agency finally walked out the door, leaving Aunt Molly with a stack of stuff to read.

Mattie had listened to every word those grown-ups said, but she was still confused.

"Aunt Molly, what's going on?"

Molly rubbed her hands against her white apron, watching the cars back out and pull onto the highway. "Well, kiddo, it turns out you were right. That stuff across the road might be dangerous. Until they figure out how much of it was dumped and where it's leaked,

I have to keep Owl's closed. They might shut down the campground too. And they've notified all the neighbors with wells. I might even have to pay for cleanup. And there's something in these papers about daily fines for unresolved violations."

"That's not fair," Mattie said, glaring out the window.

"Why would you have to pay to clean up somebody else's gloop, Ms. Waters?" Sasha asked.

Mattie looked at Sasha sideways, but it was a good question.

"Well, that's just it," Aunt Molly said. "They think that gloop is from *my* kitchen. They think it's old fryer oil, because of the smell. They think I dumped it because I didn't want to pay to have it disposed of properly. And unless I can prove I didn't, we've got to clean it up."

Beanie pointed at Aunt Molly. "You weren't even a suspect!"

Mattie's brain whizzed like a donut fryer spitting hot oil. Pop. Sizzle. Fizz. How could anybody believe that Aunt Molly would do something like this?

Mattie snuck another look at her friend. Sasha was spitting mad. So mad she looked like she might smack somebody. Her arms were crossed, and her pokey elbows jutted out like broken branches.

But was she mad because the shop had to close?

Or did she think that Aunt Molly was the glooper?

"Don't worry, Ms. Waters," Sasha said. "Nobody will believe you did it. We'll catch those gloopers."

Aunt Molly sighed, walked to the door, and turned over the sign that had the shop's hours on one side. "I don't know, girls," she said, flipping the deadbolt with a loud and very final click.

The back of the sign listed the shop's hours. Open every day from 6 a.m. to 5 p.m. It wasn't even ten in the morning. Aunt Molly couldn't close for the day.

If they weren't selling donuts, how would they pay those cleanup fines?

And what about Mrs. Mantooth's always wanting improvements on the well or the driveway? If the county sent her a letter about the well, Mattie knew Mantooth would go into attack mode and want everything tested and changed. How would they pay for all *that*?

Owl's couldn't close.

If Aunt Molly wasn't running the donut shop . . . what would she and Mattie do?

Mattie sped across the kitchen and banged through the metal door out back. She stomped through the flowerbed alongside the shop before passing the front windows again. Something beside the notice of closure caught her eye.

Owl's Outstanding Donuts. Sorry, We're Closed. See You Again Soon!

The official-looking signs from the health department and the Monterey Environmental Services Agency were one thing, but staring at Aunt Molly's cheerful pink *Closed* sign, flipped forward when it shouldn't be, was another. The sight made Mattie feel sticky and sour inside. Not another donut would get made in the kitchen of Owl's Outstanding Donuts that day.

THE BOYSENBERRY BEAUTY
A LIME-ZEST-SPRINKLED CAKE DONUT WITH BRIGHT BOYSENBERRY ICING AND PISTACHIO CRUMBLES

Aunt Molly kept up the *Closed* sign up for the next three days, which had never happened in the whole history of the Waters family. Whenever Mattie looked toward the ditch, the hazard tape flickered in the wind like the ghost of a giant mutant banana slug. She wished the gloop really had come from something like that. Something made up.

Thursday, the day after the shop shut down, Mattie borrowed Beanie's binoculars and searched for the owl. She stood under the giant redwood tree, surrounded by ferns and sprinkle-filled owl pellets. She hooted deep and low.

But the owl didn't come down or visit her trailer.

And it didn't hoot back.

She hadn't even heard him at night lately.

Mattie guessed the owl had gotten what he wanted from her. Nobody would be dumping gloop into the creek anymore. After all, the sheriff's department had caught on. The gloopers would be crazy to come around again. Owl's was closed, but she guessed the owl didn't care about that.

Mrs. Mantooth sure didn't care about Aunt Molly's troubles either. When she opened a notice from the county about the dumping, she marched straight over to bang on the door to their trailer. She must have noticed the red sign posted in Owl's front window, must have known money was about to get tight for Aunt Molly, but she didn't say a word about it. Her pestering about the well pump exploded into demands and threats. Mattie hid her head under her pillow, but she could still hear every word.

And Mattie knew she couldn't hide forever.

She had to do something.

On Friday, she snuck along the trail that skirted Mrs. Mantooth's property. She'd decided to follow it southeast, until she reached the high wooden fence that hid Hermit Harriet's house from view. She didn't want to admit that Sasha could be right about Harriet. She didn't really want the hermit to be a suspect. But Mattie couldn't rule her out.

Once Mattie reached the high fence, she found a crooked oak tree that leaned close to the fence and shimmied herself into the tree's branches. From up there, she had a view of Harriet's place. And she was pretty sure that the scrubby oak branches would keep her mostly out of sight.

Harriet's house was an old cabin. Plain but pretty. Her white truck was parked perfectly in line with a tiny shed where Harriet did all her carpentry. The shed door was open, but the interior was dark. Mattie couldn't tell if the shed's walls were empty or crammed full of tools.

Everything was quiet.

Until out of nowhere a circle saw screamed up into the air. Mattie flinched in the tree. Then, in a noisy whoosh, about ten turkeys came flying out of the scrub to land on the top of the fence. They gobbled at the screaming from the shed like a family of neighbors complaining about noise.

The trespassing turkeys looked silly perched there on the fence. The big blue-headed tom gobbled so hard he nearly fell. And soon enough Harriet Hargrave stopped her sawing and came out to glare at them. Her dark eyes glinted under her patchy gray eyebrows. Mattie wasn't sure if Harriet was one of those people who'd shoot a wild turkey and eat it for dinner. But she looked like she might be.

Mattie ducked back behind the prickly oak branch and dropped out of sight.

Okay. Hermit Harriet was definitely still on the list.

When Saturday morning came, Aunt Molly still didn't have any donuts in the case. No Chocolate Rainbows.

No Golden Galaxies. Not even the plain Old Fashioned Owls. Still, Molly was at Owl's, same as always, this time scrubbing it from top to bottom. After Mattie said good morning, Molly shooed her off and told her to have some cereal. Cereal!

Mattie let herself out the back of the shop but paused when she saw a beat-up tan Corolla slide into the parking lot. A man stepped out, and Mattie's heart dropped. It was Mr. Slug, coming for a donut. It wasn't even Sunday, so he couldn't be there expecting Slug Bars. He walked quickly to the front of the shop, peering at the notices slapped into the windows.

For a flicker of a second, Mattie wondered if the man could help somehow. He'd been a friend of Grandma's, after all.

"We're closed," Mattie said.

"I heard, but I had to come see for myself." He brushed his hands down the front of his yellow-checked shirt, looking flustered. Like his day was ruined.

"I'm sorry if that messes up your weekend," Mattie said. "I know you like the Sunday special. I'm sure we'll have Slug Bars for sale next week. Like usual."

"Of course you will," Mr. Slug said, but his eyes flicked over to the notices in the window again. He didn't actually look like he believed her. "Lillian would . . ."

Mr. Slug shook his head with a hard look in his eyes and didn't finish.

Mattie guessed he couldn't.

She turned and headed back to the trailer. She didn't want to watch him drive away or ask him for help he probably couldn't give. It would be too sad. What if there were never any Sunday Slug Bars again? Grandma Lillian would certainly have wanted Mattie and Aunt Molly to do everything they could to make sure that didn't happen. But . . . Mattie wasn't sure she could.

She would do *almost* everything.

Just not the one thing that might help the most.

Later that Saturday morning, Sasha and Beanie came over. Mrs. Little had asked them to go play somewhere else so she could get everything ready for Beanie's birthday party. They brought bagels. Mattie nudged hers aside, not wanting to ask where they came from. The three girls sat cross-legged on Mattie's bed.

Sasha took a giant bagel bite and licked some cream cheese off her thumb. Mattie's stomach gurgled. Fine. She unwrapped her own bagel and took a bite. It was good. No way as good as a donut but better than a bowl of cereal.

Sasha kept saying all they had to do was get on that bus, hop off when they got to Monterey, and take her camera to the drug store. Then they could maybe clear Molly's name.

Mattie tried convincing Sasha that they should

send the click-camera by mail instead.

"No way," Sasha said. "Right on their website, they say that they are *not responsible for lost or damaged photographs.* This is our only proof. We can't put it in the mail!"

Sasha crossed her arms.

Mattie knew she was right.

She just wished there was another way.

"What if those pictures are too blurry to prove anything?" Mattie said, feeling queasy. "The guy from the disposal company already told officials from the county that Aunt Molly dumps her oil with them twice a week, the right way. But that didn't even help. She still has to pay all these cleanup fees, because our shop is right here and there aren't any other suspects. Plus Mrs. Mantooth is making a huge deal about getting the well water tested."

Mattie pulled at a stray thread from her duvet cover: a purple embroidered butterfly that had been slowly unraveling all summer. As she tugged, the last lavender strand came away.

"I'm starting to think maybe it *was* Mrs. Mantooth again," Mattie said. "Maybe she's not just after a new well. Maybe it's some weird plot to make Aunt Molly sell her land. She hates sharing her driveway with the donut shop. It definitely could be her." She shook her head. "But maybe it's not. We have to find out who *really* did it."

Sasha gave Mattie a you-know-we-have-no-choice look, but she didn't say anything about Monterey. She was still waiting, all patient and smug and sure.

"I bet you the owl knows something," Mattie said. She could just see the big scraggly redwood out her window.

Why wasn't that owl helping?

Was it mad at her?

Where was he?

"Maybe the owl was just hooting to hoot when you woke up that first time," Sasha said. She hadn't gone back to saying that Mattie was lying about the owl, but it was kind of obvious that she thought Mattie had at least dreamed that part.

"Maybe the flowerpot and the clump of gloop are just coincidences," Sasha continued. "That makes more sense, Matt."

But *nothing* made sense.

Sasha and Beanie crinkled up the empty tinfoil from their bagels, hopped off Mattie's bed, and went home to get ready for Beanie's birthday party that afternoon.

At the birthday party, about a dozen kids from Sasha and Beanie's school—Mattie's school too, in a few days—were playing on the basketball court at the Littles' campground. Mattie already knew most of them. Pacific

Valley Elementary was pretty small. But seeing the kids made her feel less and less sure she was really going to be able to board the school bus on Tuesday morning.

Sofi, one of the other almost fifth-grade girls, smiled and said hi when Mattie arrived. The bright purple of her shirt looked like the icing on one of Aunt Molly's Boysenberry Beauty donuts, which made it hard for Mattie to smile back. So Mattie mostly stared at her shoes. Sofi's mom nudged her daughter, like come-on-you-can-say-more, but Sofi squirmed and said she was going to get some chips.

Then Sofi's mom and somebody else's dad looked at Mattie and sighed. Mattie could tell Sofi's mom was getting ready to say something. About how sorry she was about Mattie's mom or maybe just about how excited she was that Mattie would be starting school with Sofi and Sasha and Christian.

Which felt kind of like the same thing.

Mattie escaped before either could happen. She sidled up to the snack table and stuffed her mouth with chips and guacamole. A couple of seats away, Sofi grabbed a chip, dipped it, and shoved the whole thing in too. They crunched next to each other, not saying anything. Which was okay.

Better than the weird things grown-ups think they have to say.

Then there was a hula-hoop contest. That saved Mattie from figuring out how to do something with Sofi besides crunch tortilla chips. And after about an hour of silly party games, Mrs. Little brought out a cake with blue frosting covered in sour jelly beans. Everyone but Beanie thought it looked pretty gross, but Aunt Molly had made it to match an old drawing that Beanie had made of her *dream* cake. Mattie didn't glare at Christian, even though he came to the party and sat on the other side of Sasha when they sang happy birthday.

As Mrs. Little cut the cake, Mattie noticed a few of the grown-ups whispering to each other at the edges of the party. Were they making fun of the weird cake Aunt Molly made? Mattie's neck got warm. She wanted to explain about Beanie's drawing. Maybe Mrs. Little should have said something. But then her neck got hotter. Those parents were probably whispering about the shop being closed, not a silly cake.

Mattie didn't blame Aunt Molly for not coming.

Surrounded by those kids from the Big Sur school, Mattie wished she felt excited about fifth grade. This was it. She'd wanted to be with these kids, with Beanie and Sasha and Christian and Julian and Sofi and that little kid that everybody called Booger, but now she didn't care. Not with Aunt Molly's shop shut down. What would happen if Owl's couldn't reopen?

Beanie started opening her presents. Curled ribbons went whizzing through the air, wrapping paper ripped, cards were discarded. But the party didn't feel like fun to Mattie.

After Beanie lifted up her final gift, a Magic 8-Ball, Mr. and Mrs. Little each grabbed an armful of shredded wrapping paper and boxes to cart off to the closest recycling bin. The other kids started playing a game with Beanie's new squirt guns, and Mattie slipped away from the basketball court, collecting a handful of ribbons and tissue paper on her way out. She drifted toward the Littles' recycling bin, on the deck behind their cabin kitchen.

Mrs. Little didn't hear her come up the path.

She and Mr. Little were squishing all the wrapping paper down into the bin by the kitchen door.

Mattie hovered at the edge of the deck steps.

"If she has to stay closed past Labor Day, I can't see how Molly's going to make it," Mrs. Little said. "Not on top of those fees. Even without them, it'd be rough. I figure Molly's only got enough in the bank for the new well pump *or* the cleanup fees. Not both. And Monday's her biggest day of the year until Memorial Day. If she misses it . . ."

Mattie pressed her back against the slats of the deck stairs, trying to breathe more quietly. Her handful of ribbons and tissue paper wasn't making the quiet thing that easy, but Mattie was starting to feel like an expert at snooping.

Monday was two days away. She had to do something to help Aunt Molly before then. If she didn't, Owl's might be closed for good. How could that be?

"She told me that real estate agent came sniffing around again," Mrs. Little continued.

"Molly should take the offer," said Mr. Little.

Mattie heard Mrs. Little gasp. "She should *not*." It was nearly a shout. Mattie could imagine Mrs. Little standing with her arms crossed and nodding her head with every word, just like Sasha.

Mattie left her scrunched-up armload of ribbons and tissue paper in a quiet pile near the deck steps. Of course Adelaide Sharpe had decided to stick her nose into things. But Mattie hadn't thought Aunt Molly would ever take the real estate lady's offers seriously.

She scanned the trees, searching for orange polka-dot eyes and gray feathers. Nothing. Well, not nothing: two jays and a funny crested titmouse. In the distance, she heard a turkey gobble. But no owl.

She heard all the kids over at the party. Saw Beanie whapping Christian over the head with a new pool noodle. Everybody was laughing. Even Sasha.

So Mattie went home.

She wondered if she should just tell Aunt Molly about the disposable camera, even though Sasha didn't want to get in trouble for being out on the highway. But what if there was nothing good in those pictures? Or . . . nothing bad? Nothing in focus?

Sasha would be in trouble. Mattie wouldn't have a best friend. And Aunt Molly would have gotten her hopes up. For nothing.

She needed to find Aunt Molly and ask her about Adelaide Sharpe. That was the next step. Mattie had to know more about this new offer. Even if she was a little afraid of what she'd find out.

THE VELVET VAMPIRE
A BLOODRED BUTTERMILK CAKE DONUT LACED WITH FANG-WHITE CREAM CHEESE ICING

Back at the donut shop, there was only one car in the parking lot. A ladybug-red Fiat. As Mattie crossed the blacktop, the door to the shop opened. Which was weird, because Aunt Molly still had the closed sign up.

Mattie hovered at the edge of the shop, peeking around the corner.

Adelaide Sharpe slid out the donut shop door, wearing a silky blue shirt with a floppy bow tied around her neck. Aunt Molly followed her outside, and Adelaide adjusted a leather folder in her hands. Adelaide Sharpe always ordered a Velvet Vampire donut. She was the kind of person who thought they were hiding their craftiness behind pure white icing, sleek clothes, and a shiny smile, but Mattie saw it easy.

She'd always thought that Aunt Molly had seen it too.

Mattie had been so worried about suspects that she hadn't worried about people like Adelaide. Too fancy to be a glooper, she thought, but still their own kind of sneaky. Always hanging around and waiting for you to crack.

Adelaide smiled, and her teeth were shiny and perfect. "Just let me know how you want to proceed," she said, hovering beside the shop door. "Call *any* time. My client's offer is truly excellent—and the timing couldn't be more perfect for you. I'd love to help you out, Molly."

Adelaide held out her card. Something Mattie had seen her do maybe ten times before. Aunt Molly usually waved Sharpe away. She never took one of those tiny white cards.

Until now.

Aunt Molly fiddled with the card and waved Adelaide off with a tight, polite smile. The real estate lady clicked across the parking lot in her shiny heels, slipped into her bright car, and swung the door shut.

As soon as Aunt Molly went back inside the shop, Adelaide Sharpe's glittery smile disappeared. Her red car eased out of its spot, but before leaving the lot, it stopped at Mrs. Mantooth's driveway. Mattie saw Mrs. Mantooth walk over and say something to Adelaide. Mattie narrowed her eyes. Why was Mrs. Mantooth hanging out in her driveway today? There sure weren't any customers to yell at. And what would Mrs. Mantooth have to say to a real estate agent?

Was *she* the client Adelaide had mentioned?

Maybe Mrs. Mantooth really was the glooper. That mess in the ditch could be a trick to shut the donut shop down. She'd have her driveway all to herself then.

Mattie yanked at the donut shop door, but Aunt Molly had already locked it. She banged on the glass until Aunt Molly's face popped up from behind the counter.

Mattie stabbed her finger toward the real estate agent's car and Mrs. Mantooth.

Aunt Molly rushed to unlock the door. But by then, the bright red car was gone and Mrs. Mantooth was peering into her mailbox like nothing had happened.

"Why are you banging on the glass, kiddo?" Molly asked. "You know better than that."

Mattie stared at the sidewalk. She was so flustered she'd never be able to explain her suspicions about Mrs. Mantooth. But that wasn't the most important thing.

"I know what you're doing," Mattie said, not meaning to say it so loud.

Not meaning to shout.

"Nice to see you too," Aunt Molly said. "What do you mean, Mattie?"

"I saw you with that lady," Mattie said. "I know why she's creeping around."

"Mattie . . . I don't know what else to do. If I take the check from Sharpe's client, I can pay all those fees. We could move the trailer, find another place to stay . . . Like Grandma always said, it's got wheels.

That's what's important. We could move the Airstream over to the campground for a bit. Mr. Little told me so. You could still go to school with Beanie and Sasha, at least for a while."

Mattie's mouth fell open.

How could Aunt Molly even think of selling Owl's? Of moving the trailer? This was where they lived. Didn't Aunt Molly remember? Mattie didn't care about school starting. Not anymore. But the donut shop was different. It was the only home she had left.

"Just don't do it," Mattie said.

"Mattie . . ." Aunt Molly started, but Mattie didn't want to listen.

She turned and ran across the parking lot, into the trailer, slamming the door behind her so hard the sound echoed through the trees. So hard that even a sleeping owl could hear it.

Once the hazard tape went up, Alfred had sworn he wouldn't involve himself any further. His greatest concern had been the river. That was solved rather neatly. Rain hadn't washed the sticky ooze into the Big Sur River just yet, and the bustle below his roost made him certain all would be handled well before the next storm.

The true culprits had not been caught, and this did

tug at Alfred's sense of justice. But his home was no longer in jeopardy.

And then things began to look bad and worse for the proprietor of the donut shop. Alfred was admittedly fond of her strawberry iced donuts, but did that warrant risking his life and privacy? No. Not in the slightest. The remaining bakeries within his range left out other passable sweets.

But . . . well.

There were his unfortunate sympathies for Mattie to be considered. How on Earth he'd come to care for that awkward little girl was beyond his comprehension, his better judgment, and his dignity.

But there it was. He cared about Mattie and he couldn't stop.

He'd tried.

Alfred had watched the girl's aunt flipping through tall stacks of papers late into the night. Watched her count and recount the contents of the money drawer. He'd guessed the shop was teetering upon collapse. The look on her face through the window said as much. And his heart went out to her. But he had not been swayed.

He'd heard Mattie and Sasha arguing about their plans—buses, photographs, things far beneath an owl's concern. And he had not been moved. He was intrigued, and that was all. The midnight misdeeds were over, he told himself. But then he overheard an argument of another sort. Mattie's voice carried perfectly across the parking lot. Her anguish echoed into his hiding place, and he felt ashamed at having hidden. Thinking of the girl and her trailer moving away was too much. Once the wheels started rolling, those trailers never came back.

When the slam from the trailer door reached the tree where he was hiding, Alfred decided that Mattie's troubles had somehow—maddeningly—become his as well. Something had to be done.

He opened his eyes all the way, determined not to let the sunlight bother him. For days, he'd been tucked inside a hole in one of the cypress trees above the trailer. Aside from the few times, late at night, when he'd ventured forth to stretch his wings and keep a general eye on things, he had spent these days listening. Moping. Thinking. Alfred squeezed himself through the craggy opening, stretched his stiff talons, and shivered his feathers into place. He swooped down to the trailer's deck.

Thump.

Mattie needed his help. And since she'd marched straight into his home at their last meeting, he marched across the wooden deck toward her trailer door and tapped, very gently, with his beak.

Tap-tap-tap.

Only silence from the trailer.

Alfred swiveled his head both ways, checking behind him for witnesses, and tapped again.

"Coming, Beanie," Mattie called.

Alfred fluffed his feathers in preparation. He had anticipated that Mattie would assume he was Beatrice and was determined not to let it bother him.

The deck shimmied gently under his talons.

The door swung open, and Alfred blinked up at Mattie Waters.

She did not immediately notice him. The range of Mattie's vision ended at least twelve inches above Alfred's beak. And he did blend in with the splintered pine beams exceptionally well.

"Beanie?" Mattie said, peering down the path.

Alfred, not wanting to startle Mattie, let forth the smallest and most melodic whoooo he could muster.

Mattie did jump. A little. But her look of confusion quickly disappeared.

"You came back!" she said.

Alfred's wings lifted involuntarily. The feathers around his beak puffed, and his heart swelled with relief at the sight of her. She wasn't even his own owlet. His inexplicable concern for her—oof, what a nuisance!

THE VEGAN MAPLE BACON BAR
A GIANT GLAZED MAPLE BAR SPRINKLED WITH CRISPY VEGAN BACON!

Mattie smiled. Looking straight into the eyes of an owl who has come to knock-knock on your door will do that to you. He seemed so small standing on her deck. Like a silly feathered mushroom. And she forgot about her impossible situation for the tiniest crumb of time.

Then the back door to the donut shop swung shut. The sound echoed across the parking lot. Aunt Molly had been cleaning every inch of the shop, banishing cobwebs and tile grease around the fryer. Taking inventory of the pink donut boxes and napkins. She even cleaned the ceiling. It was all she could do. Mattie watched as her aunt hefted a giant black bag of trash into the dumpster.

Would she turn around?

Was she coming home?

"Quick," Mattie said, her eyes going as big as the owl's. "Meet me under the deck."

The owl blinked, raised its feathery eyebrow thingies, and hopped around the side of the trailer.

Crump-crump-crump.

Mattie covered her mouth, trying not to giggle. Owls definitely were better at flying than hopping. The owl approached an opening in the patterned wood that closed off the space beneath the deck. It was almost like a door, but really one of the latticed panels had just fallen down a long time ago. He slipped through without hesitation.

As Mattie ducked under the deck, Aunt Molly's footsteps thudded above. The trailer door clicked open and closed.

They'd just made it.

Mattie blinked around. Shimmery slides of sunlight came through the diamond-shaped holes in the deck's wood siding. Two summers ago, Mattie had made a fort under the deck, but she hadn't been back much lately. A used carpet she'd dragged in from Mrs. Mantooth's trash pile was still tucked into her favorite corner, beside a stack of water-warped books. Crayons and plastic toys from that old summer still lined the beams, and droopy origami cranes and dragonflies hung from the bottom of the deck, mildewed and dangling from dental floss. Everything was still there, gathering dust, but it all felt smaller. The dark corners didn't feel as far away. Mattie knew she had gotten bigger since she was eight, but it was easier to imagine that the whole world had just shrunk instead.

The dark underside of the deck took her backward in time, to when she had a mother and was only on vacation. It felt nice. So different from the dark road in her dreams. This was a place she'd been before.

But even there, where everything else was the same, Mattie was not.

The owl stood aside, hopping backwards to give her more room. She settled onto the musty Persian carpet, perched on her knees, not sure how to begin. She wished they had a donut to nibble. Something big enough to share between them, like one of Aunt Molly's maple bars. That might have made things easier. There was so much to explain. So much to ask. But Mattie decided she needed to know one thing first.

"What's your name?" Mattie asked.

Mattie saw instantly that she had asked the correct question. No matter what came after, this had been the place to begin. The owl fluffed his feathers in a shivery ripple.

"Hmmm," Mattie said, giving the owl a careful look. "Is it . . . Zeus? You could be a Zeus."

The owl pressed his feathery crests down.

Not even close.

She stared into the owl's golden eyes. Dust motes glowed around him. But what if the owl wasn't a him at all? She needed to start at the beginning. Mattie scrunched her mouth, thinking of a great name for a girl owl.

"What about . . . Athena?"

The owl didn't blink. But it winked.

That sure seemed like a no . . . but also a yes. "So your name's *not* Athena."

The owl blinked. Correct.

"But, you *are* a girl?"

The owl pressed its ear tufts all the way down. Nope.

"So maybe it's a name *like* Athena. One that starts with the same letter?"

He blinked. Yes.

Mattie spouted a list of names while watching the owl carefully. "Abraham. Abel. Adonis. Albus. Ash. Andy. Alexander." She took a breath. "Alfred."

At the mention of that name, the owl's ear tufts rose in surprise. He blinked once. That was a yes!

"Alfred!" Mattie said, smiling. "I love it."

And that's when things really began. Mattie finally felt ready to ask all her questions. She pulled out her notebook and opened it to her list of suspects.

"Alfred, do you know what the gloopers look like?"

Alfred blinked yes.

"Okay," Mattie mumbled. "I'm going to read what I wrote about my suspects, and I want you to keep doing the blinky thing."

Mattie read each description and paused, waiting for Alfred's response. She went through all the strangers from the campground and every donut shop customer on the list. Each time, Alfred pressed his ear tufts flat against his head. No. No. No. Mattie even read the descriptions for Hermit Harriet and Mrs. Mantooth twice, asking

Alfred if he was sure. And it certainly seemed like he was. Mattie slumped across the rug.

"They can't *all* be a no," Mattie said.

Alfred clicked his beak.

Mattie flipped through the notebook too quickly, tearing one of the pages. Maybe Alfred was wrong. Her list was great. Maybe owls weren't good at remembering faces or outfits. Not as good as she'd hoped, anyway.

Mattie definitely didn't feel like crossing Mantooth or Harriet off the list of suspects. But maybe she was missing someone. And maybe Mrs. Mantooth would've been a yes but her accomplice wasn't on the list, and that's why Alfred said no. It was easy to have a misunderstanding, talking with an owl.

And she didn't know how to fix it.

She didn't know what to ask next.

"Alfred, this doesn't help," Mattie said, plunking onto her butt. With her elbows on her knees and her bunched-up fists under her chin, two little tears fell onto her notebook.

"I don't have anything I can tell the sheriff's department. I can't even tell them about you. That would just get me in even more trouble."

Alfred shivered from top to bottom.

It was a question, Mattie was sure of it.

His shiver said, what do you mean?

So Mattie explained.

About everything. And it was so nice to be able to

do that without being interrupted.

She explained about the disposable camera maybe having a picture on it. She explained about the real estate agent who was trying to get Aunt Molly to sell the shop. She explained about the fines and about how a donut baker like Aunt Molly would no way be able to pay them, so maybe she would *have to* sell it.

And then she explained about cars and her mom.

About not wanting to get in anything that could go so fast. How even the bus to school or Monterey felt impossible. Dangerous. But it was more than that too. She wanted to stay put. She was scared to get off that bus and not have her mom there waiting. Mattie wanted to wait in Big Sur forever.

"Sasha says if I'm brave enough to climb a hundred-foot tree, going up the highway to Monterey should be no big deal. She called me a chicken, Alfred."

Alfred clacked his beak.

"I mean she didn't actually. She said I *wasn't* a chicken. But that's how it felt. I thought maybe it would be easier to ride on that highway again once I stopped missing Mom, but I'm not sure I'm ever going to stop."

Alfred hopped closer until he was almost touching her knee with the puffiest feathers on his chest.

"Do you think I'm a chicken, Alfred?" Mattie asked.

Alfred spun his head all the way to the left and then all the way to the right, which was the silliest way to say no that Mattie had ever seen.

Mattie swiped at her cheeks and laughed. "Well, at least that's one of us. So . . . you think I should go?"

Alfred blinked, pulled his ear tufts down, and blinked again. Which Mattie took to mean: Yes, if you can. And she thought she could. Maybe.

"But what if it doesn't work? What if there's nothing in that camera?"

Alfred hopped onto the notebook and hooted a single deep note.

Whooo.

Mattie felt it tickle against her ears.

It made something hopeful hum inside her.

It made her believe that somehow things could get fixed and that she could do that fixing. She just needed to be brave enough to try.

"Okay," Mattie said, nodding. "Let's make a plan."

Half an hour later, a new plan was neatly arranged. Alfred had approved every detail. Mattie ducked back out from under the deck, hurrying beneath the cypress trees, swiping spider webs from her hair. She knew what she had to say to Aunt Molly, to Sasha and Beanie, and to Mr. and Mrs. Little. The truth. Small bits of it to each of them. Well, she could tell Sasha everything, but Mattie wasn't sure she *wanted* to do that. Or that *Sasha* wanted her to do that.

Alfred followed Mattie out, hopping through the dry leaves. Crump. Crump-crump-crump. Outside, he spread his wings, flapped, and retreated into the limbs of a sycamore. He was not altogether inconspicuous, but no one was watching.

No one but Mattie.

Once Alfred had settled onto a good perch, Mattie waved. Alfred returned the gesture, in his way, before closing his golden eyes.

"Sasha first," Mattie said quietly, marching down to the river.

She looked upstream once, to the rusty pipe that dumped into the river just where Sycamore Creek started. She wondered which way the gloop would go if rain came before the county could get it all scooped up: down the creek or down the river? Maybe both.

She splunked downstream faster but didn't slip on any rocks or get sploshes of water on her shorts. Sasha was in the first place Mattie looked for her. The blanket fort in her family's messy living room. She always liked to hide out after a big party. Mostly so she didn't have to help clean up.

Sasha peeked over the edge of her book as Mattie came into the room.

"Okay," Mattie said. "Let's do it."

"I knew you wouldn't let the donut shop get fried," Sasha said, making a tiny creased triangle at the top of the page she'd stopped on.

Flup.

The book closed.

"So what's our excuse for going?" Sasha said. "My mom's not going to say yes if we tell her we're figuring out who's behind a criminal conspiracy."

"I already thought of that," Mattie told her. "We'll say we're going to the aquarium up in Monterey. I have a free four-person pass and everything. I won it in a raffle at my old school. And we've got to say it's like practice for me. You know, riding in a bus before school starts. Plus," Mattie paused, "the free pass is about to expire, so we *have* to use it."

Sasha's eyes sparkled. "Oh, that is good. No way is my mom going to say no to a coupon."

Now Mattie was really smiling, because it was absolutely true. Free anything was Mrs. Little's secret weakness . . . or greatest strength. Mattie wasn't sure, but it didn't really matter.

"I'll go convince Aunt Molly. You go talk to your mom. Have her call Owl's in like fifteen minutes."

"Got it," Sasha said, already hustling down the hall shouting, "Beanieeeeeee!"

The line that Mattie and Sasha both agreed to use, and that Alfred had so enthusiastically endorsed, was that grown-ups would ruin the whole point of riding the bus. How could Mattie get ready to ride to school all by herself (sure, with Sasha and Beanie too) if Mr. Little or Aunt Molly tagged along? It would be too embarrassing if Mattie chickened out on the first day in front of everybody—so she had to practice. Plus she'd already done it a bazillion times, plus the coupon, so please-please-please could they go?

Mattie was at the donut shop, finishing up with her speech, when the old black phone on the wall started to ring. Aunt Molly ignored it. She didn't look convinced yet that the girls riding the bus together all alone was a stellar idea.

Her face had sprouted extra wrinkles overnight.

She was wearing her apron, but the donut case was empty. The phone stopped its rattling ring.

"Please," Mattie said. "I'll only take the girls to the aquarium. I won't let Beanie get lost. Me and Sasha . . ."

"Oh, Mattie. I know you would take care of Beanie. Nobody's worried about that. Why don't you let me take you girls? The shop's closed—"

"Aunt Molly, I have to figure out how to do this by myself. School starts on Tuesday. I want to be ready. I need to be ready."

It was easy to say because it wasn't a lie.

Owl's old black phone rang again, and this time Aunt Molly reached over and answered. "Hi Betz . . . Yep, I'm getting the same treatment here." Then Aunt Molly laughed and turned away. Her shoulders eased down from around her ears.

That was it.

They had permission!

Mattie smiled a sneaky half smile, imagining all the convincing that Sasha had done on her end. Mrs. Little's yes was maybe more important than anyone's.

"I'll pack them a lunch, and we can get them on the noon bus tomorrow with Janelle . . . Yep. She'll take care of them . . . great. Okay, bye Betz." Aunt Molly clunked the phone back onto the wall.

She looked straight into Mattie's eyes, and Mattie stood up on her tiptoes, grinning.

"We want you three wearing long pants, and you'll have to put on some real shoes for once. *That* should help you get ready for school too. We'll meet the Littles up at the bus stop tomorrow at noon. If you change your mind, nobody . . ."

"I'm never changing my mind, Aunt Molly. Not about this."

"Then scoot, kiddo—go find that pass!" Molly swatted her with a yellow dishtowel and smiled.

The worried creases on her aunt's face disappeared, creases that had been there since the donut shop closed down. Mattie hoped she'd be able to make them stay away forever.

THE CAMPFIRE CRULLER
A GENTLY GLAZED TRADITIONAL FRENCH CRULLER—AS TWISTY AS HISTORIC HIGHWAY ONE!

On Sunday, promptly at noon, Sasha and Beanie and Mrs. Little and Mattie and Aunt Molly all met at the bus stop along Highway One. The three girls were wearing stretchy leggings and zippy jackets with pockets and for-real shoes with socks and everything. Mattie's turquoise backpack was heavy with the lunch that Aunt Molly had packed. It clinked and clunked and gurgled with good things. Mattie showed the free aquarium pass off to Sasha and Beanie, and their eyes sparkled at each other with their secret hope of saving everything.

Mrs. Little gave Sasha Mr. Little's shiny new phone, which she'd commandeered for the day. She also gave Sasha strict instructions to text her three times: when they arrived in Monterey, once they were in the aquarium, and when they were on their way back. Sasha zipped it into the pocket of her jacket with a very satisfied expression.

When the county bus came bobbing around the bend, Mattie sucked in her breath. You get a little older and some things end up feeling small, like her fort under the deck, but some things just keep getting bigger. Scarier. Harder. Sasha reached for Mattie's hand but looked the other way, like they always held hands and it was no big deal. Then Sasha bumped Beanie with her hip, and Beanie quickly grabbed Mattie's other hand.

Sasha really was a great person to have on your side.

Mattie watched the bus easing closer and tried not to think about how it would feel to go so fast, tried not to think about the driverless car from her old dream. She tried to focus on the cracked disposable camera instead. She didn't know what would be waiting inside it, but she wanted to believe that whatever the camera was hiding would help her catch those gloopers and help Aunt Molly. Which would make getting on that bus worth being so scared.

As the bus got closer, Mattie didn't turn around, but she knew Aunt Molly and Mrs. Little were exchanging looks. Waiting to see if she really could do it.

Hissssss.

The bus stopped in front of them.

Pssst-clap!

The folding doors opened.

There was Janelle. Her hair was different, in braids now and twisted up into what looked like a crown. But she smiled just the same as she had all those other times, and her shiny brown cheeks made Mattie want to smile too.

"Hey, Mattie! Come on up."

Janelle waved them up the bus steps, but Mattie's feet felt glued to the ground. Stuck in black tar. Sasha squeezed her hand. Beanie tugged. Mattie's heart pounded, and she let herself be pulled up the bus steps.

Mattie looked back at Aunt Molly from the top of the bus's steps. Her aunt's face pulled into a tight smile. She looked ready to get on that bus and pull Mattie off if Mattie so much as squeaked. But Mattie knew that staying put in Big Sur wouldn't solve anything.

She'd been trying to keep herself safe. And that was okay. Losing her mom—that was something scary. But if she didn't want to lose the home she had now in Big Sur, she had to be brave. She had to stay on that bus and she had to be ready to step off in Monterey, where Mom wouldn't be waiting. If her plan didn't work out . . . she'd just have to come up with another one. Mattie gulped in a big breath and shook Sasha's hand away.

She showed Sasha and Beanie how to pay the fare.

They sat right behind Janelle, all squished together, and waved goodbye to Aunt Molly and Mrs. Little. Mattie tried to smile, but what came out was a crooked grimace. She still didn't feel very brave, but she just had to pretend. Especially sitting next to Beanie.

Creak–clack!

The doors closed.

Janelle turned around with her hand still on the

door lever. "No donut this time?" she said, raising her eyebrows. "Guess I'll let you ride, but I will say I'm surprised!"

Mattie knew Janelle was only teasing, but it still made her flinch.

She had always brought Janelle a donut from Owl's on her way home to Monterey. But now the shop was closed, and she might not *have* donuts to share anymore.

"Next time I'll bring you a Campfire Cruller," Mattie said, like it was a promise.

And it was.

It was a promise that Mattie was determined to make true, if she could.

They'd get that picture developed, and it would clear Aunt Molly. The girls would take it to the police, and then someone else would have to pay those stinky cleanup fines. The donut shop had to be open for the Monday holiday so Aunt Molly could make enough to keep the business. No way was Mattie going to let the gloopers get away with having Aunt Molly pay for cleaning up the ditch. Everything would work out.

That's what Mattie wished for, anyway, and wishing was halfway to believing it was possible.

"That cruller would be perfect!" said Janelle. "Hang on, girls. Let's get this show on the road."

The brakes on the bus hissed, Janelle grabbed the big steering wheel, and they careened around the first corner. Mattie's shoulders bumped against Sasha and

Beanie's. There was an empty swoop in Mattie's stomach as they picked up speed.

But Mattie could see Janelle sitting solidly in front of her.

The bus door was clamped shut.

And Mattie wasn't alone.

That old scary dream was gone, and when Janelle asked them what their plan was up in Monterey, they explained about the aquarium while sharing sneaky smiles with each other. The swoopy feeling in Mattie's stomach began to disappear.

Sasha's smile was in charge and super certain.

Beanie's smile was honestly just about the aquarium, because she'd forgotten all about their secret plan in her excitement over seeing for-real jellyfish.

Mattie's smile was a little different. She was glad to finally be on the bus. She'd done it, and now she thought the yellow bus was going to be no problem when school started on Tuesday. Which was only in *two* days. So her smile was proud but also a little uncertain.

What would happen when she got to school on Tuesday? Would the kids around her look at her weird, thinking that Aunt Molly was the glooper? Would she be able to get through the day without missing Mom? Without wanting *her* to be the one waiting at the bus stop at the end of the day? Mattie wasn't sure about that either.

Suddenly the bus bumped over a big pothole, and Beanie's little butt went flying up off the seat next to her. "Yee-haw!" Beanie said, like she was riding a wild horse and not a rumbling bus.

Janelle chuckled. "You are my kind of girl."

And Mattie stopped worrying and let her body quiver and flop into Sasha. The three girls giggled and started playing Mattie's old favorite car game. They wobbled against each other during every turn, like strawberry-flavored Jell-O, because worrying wouldn't help. She squished a giggling Beanie against the side of the bus. Things were going to be okay—Mattie could almost taste it.

THE CHOCOLATE TWIST
A TWISTED YEAST DONUT WITH A HINT OF CINNAMON AND OUR SHINY DEEP-DARK-CHOCOLATE GLAZE ON TOP

Almost an hour into Mattie's slow, twisty bus ride through the Big Sur redwoods, the rocky cliffs above the turquoise ocean became smooth brown hills dotted with fluffy yucca fronds. As Highway One turned into a freeway and Monterey loomed ahead, Mattie's stomach went queasy. It wasn't from the ride or all their snacks. They were almost there.

"I'm so bored," Beanie said. She slumped against Mattie's shoulder. Beanie was practically buried under string cheese wrappers, tangerine peels, and empty cracker boxes.

Sasha shook an empty box. "Jeez, Beanie—I can't believe you ate all that. I'm surprised you haven't barfed."

"Nobody say the word *barf*," Beanie groaned.

"*You* just said the word *barf*," Sasha said.

Beanie clutched her stomach, sending cheese wrappers and cracker crumbs flying.

"Here," Sasha snapped, handing over Mr. Little's

phone. "Send Mom a message and tell her we made it. I just saw a sign for the aquarium."

Beanie perked up. Her groaning was mostly an act—Beanie had never barfed in her entire life. Mrs. Little said she had a bionic stomach. Beanie's fingers skittered over the tiny keyboard, adding emojis and misspelling every word.

Sasha leaned over Mattie to proofread.

"Beanie! I said send Mom a message, not Ms. Waters."

Beanie jerked the phone away. "I already sent the one to Mom. I'm just telling Ms. Waters hi."

She waved the phone toward the other girls. Mattie leaned back so she wouldn't get smacked, but she did notice that Beanie had sent Aunt Molly a whole row of donut emojis along with her note about them being *olmost ther.*

Which didn't seem like the most polite thing.

The donut emojis, not the misspellings.

Mattie tried to ignore the sourness in her stomach. Aunt Molly wouldn't mind. She would know that Beanie didn't mean anything by the tiny donuts. But they reminded Mattie why she had to get this right.

Mattie scrunched in her seat, wrapping her arms around her upset stomach, which made Sasha peek over at her. Mattie tried to think of the day's plan like an adventure. It should be fun, right?

She grabbed the metal bar in front of their seat as Janelle slung the bus into the next lane, down the freeway ramp, and into Monterey. A few cypress trees clung to the edges of the city, but the sky was open and blue. The city's bay and docks and streets spread outside of the big bus windows like the top of a cake.

Mattie pointed toward the bay. Ripples of current and shadows of kelp smudged the surface of the water like they always had. "There it is."

The bus hissed to a stop, and its doors creaked open. Janelle shifted around on her seat to wave them off. "You two follow Mattie. She knows what's good."

Then the doors clapped closed again, and the bus eased off down the street.

Mattie peeked down at her shoes, standing there on the Monterey sidewalk. The bus to Monterey hadn't careened around the corners out of control, hadn't crossed any double yellow lines and crashed. Mattie was safe, but all around her the open sky echoed with the truth.

Mom wasn't here.

Mom wasn't anywhere.

Knowing that was still scary, but she couldn't let being afraid steal her home—the home she had now, with the donut shop and their trailer and a feathery, friendly owl—away from her. So when Beanie hopped up and down, asking, "Which way, which way?" Mattie was ready to show her.

Sasha was glaring at the map on her mom's phone, trying to figure out the directions. Mattie peeked over her shoulder, then pointed at the real street.

"The aquarium is that way," Mattie said. "But we've got to do the click-camera thing first, Beanie."

"Ahhhh. I forgot." Beanie flopped her arms and let her shoulders slump.

Sasha squinted at the phone. "So if the aquarium is that way"—she turned the phone around in her hands, and the picture flipped—"then the pharmacy is . . ."

She pointed.

Mattie nodded.

Beanie skipped ahead.

Sasha zipped the phone back into her pocket.

It was kind of nice walking on actual sidewalks, but it felt strange too. The trees didn't crowd close together in Monterey like they did in Big Sur. Things were open and straight and blue, not curvy and close and green. The whole city felt bigger but not fuller. Easier to get around but not an easier place to be. Mattie didn't quite know how to put those feelings into words. So she didn't. When they got to her old street, Mattie couldn't see the house that wasn't hers anymore. But it was just over the rise. Two blocks away. That was it.

The house tugged at her. Knowing it was there made Mattie want to make a whole new plan. But that house wasn't what she was trying to save.

Mattie's feet pulled her along, and pretty soon the girls were standing in front of the springy automatic doors of the big drug store. They walked in together, and whoosh! The place swallowed them up.

Rectangular lights blazed between the dotted ceiling tiles. The cash registers bopped, and the conveyer belts scooted candy and shampoo and bandages toward the rows of employees in scratchy-looking green vests.

Sasha and Mattie scanned the signs hanging above the maze of aisles. Pharmacy, first aid, cosmetics, hair care . . .

"There," Sasha said, grabbing Beanie's hand.

Mattie's skin prickled when she read the red-and-white sign: *Photos and Prints*. This was it!

They hustled toward the faraway aisle, ignoring the teetering stack of red shopping baskets and the grinning uniformed greeter. The little counter of the photo section was almost as full of things as the kiosk at the campground. A stand with batteries and gift cards, a tray of gum, and a bunch of miniature umbrellas that nobody would need for months.

There was a silver bell at the edge of the only empty space.

Sasha reached her hand forward and smacked it with confidence.

A teenager using too much make-up to cover a pimple on her forehead leaned forward. She was sitting on a stool, scrolling through her phone and chewing on a piece of gum. Mattie knew Mrs. Little would be horrified. She did not approve of gum. The girls only got to chew gum at parties, never in the house.

"Yeah?" said the girl, not looking up from her phone.

Sasha pulled the click-camera out of her pocket and placed it in the center of the counter.

Beanie grabbed a massive bag of sour jelly beans. "Let's get these too—I'm hungry!"

Sasha ignored the jelly beans, crossed her arms, and stared down the teenager. "My dad said you can get these things developed in an hour."

But Mattie was starting to get a bad feeling about their plan.

The teenager behind the counter snorted. Really. And she laughed with her head thrown back, but all quiet, so she wouldn't get in trouble with her supervisor. "Sure, you could get it done in an hour . . . like a decade ago."

She hitched up her too-tight pants, pulled at her green vest, and tapped at a little sign with her short painted nails.

The nails were magenta and shimmery.

Kind of like a strawberry-glazed donut with sprinkles.

Mattie stared at those nails, mesmerized, thinking they must be a sign from the universe or something. Because right then, she really needed one. Because the actual sign that girl had been tapping made it clear that the pharmacy could no way get those pictures out of their busted-up camera within an hour.

"Can I still get the jelly beans?" Beanie huffed, shaking the bag in front of Sasha's face.

Sasha was turning red.

Sasha Anastasia Little did not enjoy being wrong.

Or being laughed at.

And that teenager behind the counter was about to get an earful.

THE CARDAMOM CLASSIC
A SIMPLE CAKE DONUT WITH A MODERN TWIST—GENTLY SPICED WITH TOASTED CARDAMOM AND ICED WITH A MATCHA GREEN TEA GLAZE

Even though Sasha went all Mrs. Little on the girl behind the counter, super huffy and in charge, spewing words like *incompetent* and *corporate liars* and *false advertising*, nothing she said could convince the older girl that the drugstore did indeed provide one-hour photo development.

"We need to talk to your manager," Sasha finally said, smacking the counter.

The girl wouldn't stop laughing.

"Hang on, can you say that again?" she said, holding up her phone. "I want to Snapchat it."

Sasha crossed her arms, refusing to say another word.

"Look, Minizilla," the teenager said, sliding her phone into her pocket, "you can put the camera in this little envelope, and we'll send it off to get developed. Takes seven to ten days."

She shoved the envelope across the counter.

Sasha and Mattie looked at each other and then read the fine print.

"Not responsible for lost or damaged film," Sasha whispered.

"Ten days is too long. We need it *today*." Mattie pushed the envelope back toward the girl. Her mind felt fizzy.

Beanie butted her head in between them both, shaking the bag of jelly beans. So Mattie bought them, and the three girls drifted away from the counter defeated.

The drugstore doors spit them out onto the sidewalk. Mattie snuck a look at Sasha. She was still furious. Still stumped. What were they going to do now? The thing about the teenager's pink, shiny nails poked at Mattie's brain.

It *was* a sign.

"Follow me," Mattie said, feeling like she'd been woken up from a dream.

Beanie obviously thought they'd given up on the camera plan and were heading to the aquarium, because she was bouncing again. She didn't really get that they were all about to lose the donut shop forever and maybe each other. Sasha was still stumped and confused, but she trotted along following Mattie. She didn't interrupt.

"Pink . . ." Mattie mumbled as she sped down the sidewalk, turning a corner. "Pink, pink, pink!"

Mattie pointed.

At a sign.

A pink sign that shimmered in the bright sun, round as a donut and hanging above a shop door. It said, *Otto's Fine Photography*. Mattie had walked by it a million times with Mom on their way down to the aquarium or to the pharmacy. It had been there forever. Just waiting for them. For her.

Sasha didn't look so sure.

She scrunched her mouth and peeked in the front window.

There were a few giant prints of sunsets and the ocean and fog-covered redwoods. Arty stuff. Fancy looking. Expensive.

"I don't know, Matt," she said. "I guess we could try."

"Trust me," Mattie said. "I've got a good feeling about this place."

And it was true. Mattie did have a good feeling, a feeling that pulled her feet toward the shop. But she also had a secret whisper of worry. It told her that the pictures wouldn't help. It told her that Aunt Molly's donut shop would never open again. It told her they'd have to leave home. That nothing would turn out right. Not without Mom. Mom had always been so sure and happy and positive.

Mattie wasn't certain she could be that kind of person.

But she grabbed Beanie by the hand and tugged her inside.

Determined to at least try.

The door had a bell on it. Exactly like the one on the

donut shop. Its jingle was friendly and soft. A tall, black-haired man with mottled pink cheeks stood behind the counter. His look wasn't quite as welcoming, but Mattie decided to stay positive. The man's wiry eyebrows were like weeds that hadn't been cut back in . . . well, ever. He raised them at the girls and closed the book he'd been reading with a delicate thump. Like he was a second-and-a-half away from asking where their parents were.

Mattie took a deep breath. She didn't want to give him the chance.

"Um, excuse me, can you get one of these things developed? Maybe in an hour?" She pushed Sasha forward. "Show him the disposable camera," she whispered.

Sasha bugged her eyes at Mattie, but she pulled the battered green-and-black camera from her pocket and put it on the counter. She crossed her arms and grumbled something rude about the teenager at the drugstore, which Mattie hoped that the man behind the counter couldn't really hear.

The man picked the camera up and turned it this way and that. "It's cracked, you know that?" he said.

"We *know*," Sasha said.

Mattie moved forward and bumped Sasha to the left. Just a little.

"Will it work? Can you still get the pictures out?"

The man's eyebrows twitched, reminding Mattie of Alfred's fluffy ear tufts. It was maybe like a smile, and it made Mattie want to smile back. "Would you prefer matte or gloss?" he asked.

Mattie and Beanie and Sasha all looked at each other. "Um . . . which is better?" Mattie asked. "Or, you know, clearer?"

"Ahhh, a question for the ages," the man said. "Were these photos taken in the evening or the afternoon?"

"The night," Beanie said, with her finger pointing to the sky like she was busting out a dance move.

Mattie nodded. "The *middle* of the night."

The man clutched his chin, leaning down on the counter. Mattie could tell he was pleased to be asked. She could tell he had all sorts of quiet opinions about all sorts of things. She smiled crooked and wondered what kind of donut he might get at Owl's.

She decided on a Cardamom Classic.

And she quietly added the man to the list of people she would bring a donut to if he could help save the shop. Janelle would get a cruller. The photography man would get the green donut with mysterious, delicate spices. She hoped she was right. She hoped he was *able* to help.

"I think this may call for matte paper then, ducklings. Come back in precisely one hour." He wobbled his eyebrows at Sasha, who made a sort of soft snorting sound, an almost-laugh, but kept her arms crossed.

"Thank you, sir!" Mattie said. "We'll be back in an hour."

The girls tumbled out of the jingly door again.

"Why'd he call us ducklings?" Beanie asked, all confused.

Mattie shrugged. "I think because he's old."

"I think because he's creepy," Sasha said.

"Well, creepy or not, he's our only hope. Quick—we've got to send a picture from the aquarium before we lose any more time. Otherwise your mom will get suspicious."

The sisters ran after Mattie, down the pretty streets, all the way to Cannery Row. They tugged Beanie past candy shops, loud restaurants, and packed T-shirt stores until they bumped into the end of the line for the aquarium.

Mattie slipped the four-person pass into the hand of the attendant just a whisper of a second after the woman ahead of them handed over her ticket. The skinny teenage boy punched a hole in their pass and handed them a map. He didn't even look at them. Or count.

A family of impatient boys pushed them from behind.

And the girls were inside!

The great blue hall echoed with excited shouts and crying babies. An orca whale statue hung from the ceiling above them, quiet and massive. It sucked in all the extra noise. Beanie pointed and hopped.

"*Jelly*-fish, *jelly*-fish!" she chanted. Mattie and Sasha grinned, each grabbing one of Beanie's hands.

Mattie didn't need the map.

She knew the way to the jellyfish. She knew the way to everything.

Mattie hustled the girls up the escalator and into the jellyfish exhibit. They took selfies and slow-motion videos of the ghostly jellies to send to Mrs. Little. But those pictures made Mattie more nervous about the disposable camera. She was counting on there being something important in the photos Sasha snapped. She'd decided to believe and not to worry, but that was a hard thing to really do.

What if? Those words bubbled up in Mattie's brain every time she stared into the dark water of a tank for too long. *What if those pictures don't help?*

She looked into the eye of an octopus, its skin shifting from white to red. *What if Aunt Molly can't reopen the shop?* The octopus crept toward the upper corner of its tank. *What if Aunt Molly has to sell the shop to pay to clean the ditch?* The octopus closed its eye.

What if.

Mattie tried to have fun. Told herself that the strange old man with bushy owl eyebrows would help, just like Alfred had. He was developing the pictures right then. She closed her eyes for a second, trying to believe that everything would be okay. Watching Beanie bouncing and pointing at everything made it seem easy. But it wasn't.

They went to the touch tank next, to hold all the sea stars and let the gooey sea cucumbers mush through their hands. They stood in the glass tunnel while the wave machine crashed over them. Shhhhh . . . whoosh!

The thud of the water matched Mattie's nervous heart. Mattie could tell that even Sasha was impressed with the aquarium, though Sasha tried not to show it.

So Mattie knew where she wanted to take them next.

Even Sasha wouldn't be able to pretend not to love it.

They didn't have as much time as she'd thought, because of their mess-up at the drugstore. They'd need to hurry. But no way could they miss it.

Beanie and Sasha trailed behind Mattie through the long hallway that opened into a huge dark room. So dark it could have been nighttime. The blue wall in front of them wasn't the sky, but it felt almost as big. It twinkled with schools of fish that shimmered in and out of sight. It was empty. Then . . . it wasn't. A giant stingray swirled past. People whispered and gasped.

When the stingray was gone, a hammerhead shark appeared, a gray smudge becoming slowly sharper.

Mattie led the girls closer and closer to the glass wall.

Beanie squealed.

Sasha's mouth flopped open. "Whoa."

Sometimes little kids would get scared at the open ocean exhibit, but Mattie had never felt that way. Not before. This spot in the aquarium had always been Mattie's favorite. Her mom's too. When Mattie pressed her nose against the glass, the exhibit seemed to have no edges. No bottom or top. It was all empty blueberry-colored water one second and a swirling kaleidoscope of fish the next. You never knew.

Mattie looked behind her, into the carpeted bleachers that lined the room. She couldn't see the faces of the adults all lined up there in the dark.

Mom used to sit in the back of the exhibit and work, reading briefs on her phone or answering emails. She would let Mattie watch the open ocean exhibit as long as she wanted. Then, sometimes, Mom would walk over and whisper silly things in Mattie's ear.

They had giggled.

Mattie turned away from the shadowy parents dotting the benches. Beanie and Sasha's skin looked blue in front of all that glass. Their eyes were bugged out and happy-excited. Mattie smiled and leaned close when a green sea turtle flapped toward them. She pressed her ear to the glass, like she was listening for something.

Beanie put her ear to the glass too.

"What are you doing?" Sasha said, laughing.

"Me and Mom used to hear the sea turtle say things," Mattie said. "You just have to listen. It's like a hundred years old and it can talk." This wasn't exactly true, but it was a story her Mom had liked to tell.

"Really?" Beanie squeaked.

"Shhhhh . . ." Mattie said, closing her eyes.

"Come on, Beanie," Sasha said. "Mattie's just telling a story."

"But what about the owl?" Beanie asked. "That's real, right?"

"That's just . . . I don't know. That's just different."

Beanie looked from Sasha to Mattie, like she was trying to decide who to believe, like it was a tough call. And this time, it really was.

So Beanie scrunched her eyes closed and pushed her ear as close to the glass as she could, listening for the turtle.

Mattie knew the sea turtle thing was just a story. She'd listened with *her* ear pressed against that glass for hours and never even heard a whisper. But now she felt like she could hear Mom—the whispering and the giggling. So it wasn't hard to keep her eyes closed and believe.

That believing wasn't real, but it was true. It was like a good dream with Mom in it. She didn't want to wake up or open her eyes. She'd been so afraid of riding back to Monterey, because she knew Mom wouldn't be there waiting for her like before. But here Mom was. In the dark. In the background. In the blue water at the edges of Mattie's mind.

And all her what-ifs went quiet and believing felt easier. If the photos didn't help, if Aunt Molly did have to sell the donut shop, Mattie thought they'd still be okay. Somehow. They'd figure it out.

Mattie didn't know how to explain it, but it was something she just understood.

Her eyes flicked open. The sea turtle floated closer, coming straight toward Mattie.

Sasha rolled her eyes, waiting for Mattie and Beanie to finish up.

And she waited a little longer.

And then she leaned forward and put her ear against the glass too. Just for a second.

Mattie smiled. Her hands left hot prints on the cool glass. She saw that, for the tiniest crumb of a second, both Sasha and Beanie closed their eyes.

For the tiniest second, Sasha believed too.

Beanie leaned back first. "I think I heard it!"

Mattie laughed and stepped back from the glass, looking for a bench nearby. She caught sight of the clock on some mom's phone. And her heart whooshed. "Come on! The pictures will be ready."

The sea turtle turned away, its outline blurring, but Mattie didn't wait for it to disappear.

"I really heard it, *swear*!" Beanie said, nodding a bazillion times.

"Me too," Mattie said, tugging at Beanie's hand. "It was wishing us luck!"

Sasha huffed, but she followed Mattie down the dark hall toward the entrance, and she didn't call Mattie a liar.

Not this time.

THE TART TURNOVER
A FLAKY SUGAR-CRUSTED PASTRY STUFFED WITH TART CRYSTALIZED LEMON AND CHUNKY APPLES

Just after three o'clock, with around an hour left before the girls needed to board the bus back to Big Sur, the three of them bunched up in front of the photography shop door. Mattie took a deep breath, ready for whatever the pictures had in them. But Sasha tapped the glass pointing at the closed sign. It said *Sunday: 10 a.m. – 3 p.m.*

"No way," Mattie said, pressing her nose to the glass. "This can't be happening."

"Sea turtles can talk, but *this* can't be happening. Okay. Sure."

Sasha rolled her eyes, but it was a show.

She was just as worried as Mattie.

"That guy wouldn't leave—he *knew* we were coming back," Mattie said, certain it was true. Peering into the dark shop, Mattie saw the old man with bushy eyebrows perched at his counter, nose in his book again.

She tap-tap-tapped on the door, and he turned his

head, set down his book, and waved the girls in. Mattie pushed at the door.

The bells jingled.

It was open—he'd been waiting for them.

The man put the back of his hand against his waist and waggled his bushy eyebrows at them. "You, young ladies, are late."

Mattie smiled. "Sorry. We were at the aquarium and lost track of time."

The man waved his hand toward the counter. "Your photographs are, of course, finished. They'll be $14.49. *With* tax."

Mattie led the way to the counter. Sasha, still somewhat uncertain, pulled eleven one-dollar bills and fourteen quarters from her jacket pocket. When Beanie saw all the money, her eyes went big. "Do we have enough for more jelly beans?" she asked.

The man's eyebrows quivered again. "This is not the kind of establishment that specializes in sundries, odds, or ends."

"Beanie, knock it off," Sasha said, pushing the money forward.

The man sighed and sorted through Sasha's hard-earned allowance. Mattie peeked at Sasha, who let the tiniest smile flicker at the side of her mouth before she turned back to face the stuffy cashier.

The register shuddered and spit out a small receipt. The man slid an envelope across the counter and pointed to the door. "I'm afraid we've been officially closed for"—he checked his simple silver wristwatch—"seven minutes."

"Thanks for not locking the door," Mattie said, grabbing the envelope.

She pressed it against her chest and sped out to the sidewalk. As soon as the door jingled shut behind them, Mattie heard the lock click. Right there, in the middle of the sidewalk with her heart thumping, Mattie pulled the photos from the envelope, one at a time.

The first was black as a hunk of beach tar. Nothing.

The second showed the fuzzy outline of a white truck in the darkness and two shapes that Mattie guessed were the gloopers. But the gloopers were fuzzy too. Both pictures were useless.

"Come on," Sasha said. "Look at the last one." She prodded Mattie in the side. "I took *three* pictures."

Mattie pulled out the last photograph.

A line of reflectors glinted in the foreground. The highway was shiny and black. The gloopers were blurs again, but the white truck and the drippy hose were in perfect focus. Mattie could even read the numbers on the license plate. Her heart sped up.

"5-2-1-5-1-9-N," Mattie said, tracing the photograph with her finger. "We got the license plate! This is it. This is proof. We can catch those gloopers. We can show this to Deputy Nuñez."

She felt like she was swimming in the ocean and a swell had just lifted her up.

Then she saw something else. Something familiar. Something Mattie hadn't noticed during the gloop attack. There was an emblem on the door of the truck. A logo. And she recognized it.

"You guys."

Mattie pointed.

Sasha looked closer.

Beanie wobbled on her tiptoes to see.

The logo on the side of the gloop truck had a big swirling capital *A* on it. She couldn't read the rest of the letters, but she knew what they said: *Ace's Excellent Donuts*. Mattie looked down both sides of the street, squinting.

"That gloop *was* from a donut shop, but not Aunt Molly's. I know where it is. I remember it. It's that way. Come on!"

Mattie stubbed the toe of her sneaker on a sidewalk crack, caught her balance, and hustled down the block, tugging at the edge of Sasha's jacket.

Two blocks later, the three girls slowed down.

The same logo was hanging above a little storefront. It was a donut shop for sure. Mattie could see the display case from across the street.

The girls grabbed hands, looked both ways, and zipped across the street. They peeked into the window, all in a line. The display case was smudged and mostly empty, but a few of the day's donuts were still lined up. The shop lights were off.

Closed.

Sasha poked at a flyer in the window. "Look. They've got turkey talons." But Ace's called them Otter Paws. The flyer had a picture of a sea otter floating in the bay next to a bear claw.

Mattie glared at the flyer. "Rip-offs."

"Are they good?" Beanie asked. "I'm hungry."

"I don't know," Mattie said. "Mom never let us get donuts here. She said . . . I don't remember exactly."

"Did she say that the owners were stupid criminals who deserved to go to jail and pay a bunch of fines? Because that would be a good reason not to buy their donuts," Sasha said, crossing her arms.

Mattie didn't answer, even though she agreed.

She walked down the sidewalk and poked her head into the alleyway at the edge of the shop. Over the sharp, salty smell of the bay, a tinge of garbage wafted out of a big brown dumpster. The afternoon was still warm and bright, but Mattie shivered.

At the end of the alley, a truck was parked halfway into an open garage.

A white truck.

The girls crept forward, hugging the side of the dirty wall and skirting the dumpster. They peeked around the edge of the building. The numbers on the license plate matched Sasha's photograph. The small garage was filled with teetering cardboard boxes. Through the cluttered mess, Mattie could see a silver door with the Ace's logo. "This is it," she whispered. "It's the gloop truck."

"Come on, Matt," Sasha said, tugging at her. "Let's get out of here."

Just then, the silver back door of Ace's Excellent Donuts clanged open. The girls scurried behind the dumpster. A door on the truck opened and closed a moment later, and the engine coughed itself alive. The truck backed into the alley and shuddered away, toward the street on the opposite end. When it stopped, Mattie saw the driver reach up toward the driver's-side visor and push something.

The garage door chug-chug-chugged to life, moving downward.

"Quick, they're gone," Mattie said, already heading for the garage.

"Mattie?" Sasha whispered. "What are you . . ."

Mattie ducked under the closing door. It squealed, and so did Sasha, who grabbed Beanie's hand, tugging her sister into the garage. Two seconds later, the huge door slammed against the concrete floor.

"Come on," Mattie said, slipping around a stack of boxes. She paused to twist the handle of the silver back door. It wasn't locked. With her shoulder pushing at the door, she slipped into the dark donut shop. Sasha huffed and then dragged Beanie in with her before the door clanged shut again.

The girls found themselves in a long hallway lined with three more doors. There must have been one for the kitchen, probably a supply closet, and maybe an office.

At the end of the hallway, the front windows of the shop let in a dim stream of late afternoon light. The small white tiles on the floor were dusty, with streaks of black grease. The lights hanging from the ceiling didn't have covers on them. The whole place smelled slightly of rats, a smell that Mattie knew because a family of rodents had once lived in her old hideout under the trailer deck.

"What a dump," Mattie muttered under her breath.

"Mattie," whispered Sasha. "We've got to get out of here. We don't need any more evidence."

"When we go to the sheriff's department, I have to be able to convince the deputies. That means more than just a picture in the dark. What if that truck only belongs to one of the gloopers? We need to bust them both. If I can find a picture of their faces, we could use that too. Besides, that slob's not coming back. I just . . . I just need to look around."

What Mattie needed was to understand.

Why would Ace's Excellent Donuts be dumping cooking oil into a ditch thirty miles down the road? Mattie knew she wouldn't find answers in the shop's display case, but there would have to be an office or a file cabinet somewhere.

She opened a door.

Cleaning supplies. Cleaning supplies that probably hadn't ever been opened.

Mattie opened the hall's next door and peeked in. Sasha and Beanie bumped up behind her. Inside there was a bulky desk covered in unopened mail and crumpled food wrappers. Empty coffee cups and a beat-up radio. An old leather armchair slumped behind the desk, and two folding chairs were arranged in front. Mattie wondered who on Earth would sit in them. A tall filing cabinet stood in the corner. Piles of old magazines littered the floor. But the room had no picture frames on the desk or up on its walls.

Mattie slid a file cabinet drawer open as quietly as she could.

She flip-flapped through folders and papers, not sure if anybody would keep photos in a file cabinet, but maybe she could find something else incriminating.

Chug-chug-chug. Bam! From inside the office, the girls could hear the garage door in the alley opening again. All three of them jumped.

Sasha's blue eyes went wide.

Beanie took a step closer to the bigger girls.

"What do we do?" whispered Sasha.

But it was too late to do anything.

They heard the back door's creaky handle next.

Someone was stomping down the hall, muttering and grumbling. If he found the girls going through his files, what would happen?

"Beanie, hide," Mattie said, pushing her down. "Hide right now."

Beanie scuttled along the floor and disappeared behind an especially tall stack of old magazines.

Smack. The office door flew inward.

Sasha yelped, and Mattie clutched their envelope of disposable-camera pictures close to her heart. Which she no-way should have done.

An old man with sloping shoulders and a round tummy bulging from his sweatshirt stepped into the office. He was definitely a glooper. The shorter one. Mattie recognized the shape of him and the rolling way he walked. But she also recognized him from Owl's Outstanding Donuts.

He wasn't wearing his Sunday costume, the checked yellow shirt and slacks, or ordering Slug Bars. But it was him. Mr. Slug.

He wasn't retired after all. He must not have missed her grandma's donuts the way she'd thought, either. Why had she believed that? Seeing the man for who he really was felt like flipping over a burned turnover. It might have looked all right from the top, but it was hard and ruined on the bottom. Aunt Molly tossed those right into the trash.

Mattie had been wrong. So wrong. But she didn't have time to worry about it. To feel bad or guilty. She wondered if Mr. Slug was actually named Ace, like on the donut shop sign.

"What in the—" the man growled when he saw the girls. "What did you take?"

His huge hand darted forward and plucked the envelope with the license-plate shot from Mattie's hands.

"You better believe I'm pressing charges."

"Hey! You can't do that," Mattie shouted.

Beanie's head popped out over her stack of magazines, all wide-eyed and scared, then ducked out of sight again before Ace spotted her. Mattie hoped so anyway. She knew Beanie had thought their whole investigation was a game. Until now.

Mattie watched the man's face transform while he thumbed past each photo.

Photo one: confusion.

Photo two: shock.

Photo three: anger.

The man set the pictures down and rubbed at the scruff along his neck. Mattie could tell he knew who she was. And she could tell they were definitely in trouble.

"Sit," he said, pointing to the rusty metal chairs.

Mattie and Sasha looked at each other. Sasha was vibrating with panic. A little muscle on her cheek was actually twitching.

The man lifted the receiver of an old brown phone. It had a twisty chord just like the one at Owl's. He stabbed at the sticky buttons and waited.

"We've got a situation at the donut shop. You were right. Those kids saw us. They've got a picture . . . Of course I'm going to rip it up."

Mr. Slug hung up the phone.

He leaned back in the leather armchair.

Sasha looked pokey and small and shivery in front of

the man, but Mattie didn't feel small. She felt angry. Like there was a whole universe of mad swirling in her. This grubby guy, this glooper, wasn't going to take anything away from her. He wasn't smarter or nicer or even much bigger than she was. She'd believed he was some nice man who missed someone, just like her.

He'd tricked her, but that wasn't her fault. It was his.

Mattie grabbed the edges of the cold metal chair and snuck a sideways look at the corner where Beanie was hidden away. She could only see one floof of Beanie's brown hair peeking over the stack of magazines.

Then the alley door squealed open.

"Ace?" called a woman's voice.

"In the office," Ace growled, leaning back in his armchair.

Click-click-click. Somebody gracefully slunk toward the office in high heels.

The door swung inwards, and the Velvet Vampire woman oozed into the room. It was that real estate agent. Adelaide Sharpe. The one who was trying to get Aunt Molly to sell the shop. She was wearing another skirt and silky shirt, plus a tightly buttoned-up blazer.

Adelaide Sharpe was the other glooper.

Mattie's stomach swirled.

She burped.

How could she have missed it? Mattie had been worried that Adelaide's shiny smile would tempt Aunt Molly into selling the shop, sure. But she'd never thought

Adelaide Sharpe could be a glooper. Not even when Sharpe had stopped to talk to Mrs. Mantooth.

"The photos," Adelaide snapped.

Ace handed over the three pictures.

Adelaide flipped through them way faster than Ace had, one-two-three.

She didn't let anything show on her face, but when she got to the last photo, she ripped it into eight tiny pieces.

Every scrup of tearing paper made Sasha and Mattie flinch.

"It's over. You're too late," Adelaide said. "Your aunt signed the papers."

Adelaide tossed the little photo scraps into the ashtray on Ace's desk. Then she snatched up the white envelope from the photography shop and pulled out the little brown and black negatives, crushing them into a little ball.

Plunk. She dropped them into the ashtray too.

"Burn them," Adelaide said.

THE POWDERED PUFFIES
PIPING HOT BEIGNETS LOADED WITH
FLUFFY POWDERED SUGAR AND SERVED
WITH LOCALLY SOURCED WILD RASPBERRY JAM

Mattie's eyes went blurry, but she wouldn't let the tears out. All their proof was ripped up and crumpled. Aunt Molly had already sold the shop. Everything she'd done—staking out the highway, riding that bus—was for nothing. She'd failed.

She couldn't look at Sasha or check on Beanie.

Adelaide Sharpe glared at the girls like she was waiting for something.

"You . . . you lied to her," Mattie said, trying to catch her breath. "You tricked Aunt Molly."

Adelaide laughed. "Sweetheart, I told her a story. That's what I do. It's up to her to believe it or not."

Adelaide's practiced shiny smile was gone. It was as much of a costume as Mr. Slug's Sunday shirt.

You're too late. Your aunt signed the papers.

Mattie turned Adelaide's words over in her mind like little rocks in a riverbed. They didn't feel right. They didn't sound true. Maybe Aunt Molly had signed those papers, but maybe she hadn't. And no way was Mattie too late to help.

She listened to the whisper of Mom that she had inside herself. Adelaide's story was just a fancy lie. Even *she* didn't believe it. And Mattie knew what to believe in: donuts, Big Sur, Aunt Molly.

Adelaide smoothed her skirt. "There's nothing you can do, Ms. Waters. Your photos are toast." Adelaide nodded at Ace, and he set them on fire in his gross old ashtray.

Seeing those pictures curl into blue flames made part of Mattie curl in on itself too. But that's just what Adelaide wanted. Mattie hadn't puzzled out what was really going on, but she certainly wasn't going to give up. She wasn't going to let being afraid get in the way of helping Aunt Molly. So she listened, catching Sasha's eye.

"I talked to a few people about this girl. Nobody's going to believe her, Uncle Ace. All we have to do is tell them she's lying and her little friends are trying to cover for her. The donut shop is ours, and we can tear it down and get that new hotel humming."

Mattie's eyes went wide. Uncle Ace? The rocks in her brain started to make sense. Started to make a pattern.

Mr. Slug, Ace, leaned back in his chair. He rubbed at his bristly neck again. He didn't look so convinced. "If you say so, Addie. You're the one with the know-how. Should we call the cops? Report the break in?"

"Not just yet," she said.

Mattie glanced at the office door. Adelaide took a tiny step toward her in those clicky heels, like she was ready to head Mattie off if the girls made a run for it. Maybe Adelaide was just stalling. Maybe Aunt Molly hadn't signed the papers but was about to, and Adelaide wasn't going to let Mattie go until the deal was finished.

Mattie glared at the two gloopers in turn.

Ace seemed to believe Adelaide, seemed to *think* everything was settled. But maybe Adelaide was telling him a story too, even if he was her uncle. They were working together. That much was clear. But Mattie still didn't understand why.

Mom had never let Mattie have a donut at Ace's—or go there at all—which made Mattie think that no way was he an old baker friend of Grandma's like she thought. Then again, Aunt Molly always smiled and joked with Ace when he came to order his slug bars on Sundays. She never lost patience with him pestering her about the recipe. But maybe she didn't really know about him. Or maybe she thought Mattie wasn't old enough to know. If some old feud was brewing, Aunt Molly wouldn't have wanted Mattie to worry. Still, why would somebody go to so much trouble to ruin another person's life? Aunt Molly had never done anything to anyone. Mattie was sure of that too.

"Why did you do it?" Mattie blurted out.

"Mattie, just be quiet, okay?" Sasha said. "They're letting us go soon. Right?" Sasha pleaded with her eyes. Her right cheek was still twitching.

"Listen to your friend, Mattie," Adelaide said, smirking. "Looks like she's the smart one."

But Mattie didn't think the gloopers were going to just let them go, and she couldn't just be quiet. She had to know.

"Aunt Molly never did anything to you or your crummy donut shop," she said.

Now Ace really did smile. Grinned, actually. His teeth were yellow and chipped. "Your Aunt Molly," Ace grunted. "She should never have had that shop. Should never have sold those Slug Bars. They were my idea. Mine." He slapped his big, bear-claw-sized hand on the table, and all the trash jumped away.

"Your grandmother," Ace said, pointing a stubby finger across the desk, "was a treacherous woman. A liar. She knew those Banana Slug Bars were *my* idea! And she ran off with Herman *Waters* and started her own shop. She threatened to take me to court if I didn't stop selling Slug Bars here. She called them knock-offs." Ace's bald head turned red and his nose was basically purple. He looked dangerous.

But Mattie almost laughed.

He was *jealous*.

"So, how'd you think them up then?" she asked. "What gave you the idea?"

Ace blustered, his head turning redder around its powdered-sugar ring of hair. "I just did," he said. "I had the idea. She stole it. That's all."

Mattie knew Grandma's story about the slug bars. She'd heard it a hundred times. Grandma had been at some music festival up in Monterey in the spring. While she was lying on the grass, enjoying the music, she saw a bright banana slug slime its way across a plain old-fashioned donut lying on a napkin under a grove of redwood trees.

Grandma said it was like the slug was dancing in slow motion.

She said she told all her friends at the festival about her idea for a donut shop with banana-slug-shaped bars. Everyone had laughed except for Herman Waters. Well, he'd laughed, but he also told her it was a good idea.

So they got married.

And they opened a donut shop on the land that Herman's great uncle had left him down in Big Sur.

That was a story that felt true to Mattie.

None of Ace's red-faced blustering made Mattie doubt it.

If he'd come up with the slug bar idea, then he wouldn't have been pestering Aunt Molly for the recipe after all these years. Mattie would bet that he'd never come up with a good idea in his life. Maybe not even a bad one. She snuck a peek at Adelaide. The bad ideas were that lady's job. All Ace had was a grimy, gross, empty shop. He was jealous of Grandma Lillian's ideas and Grandpa Herman's love and Aunt Molly's hard work.

Mattie had plenty of ideas and plenty of love. Just like Aunt Molly and Mom and Grandma and Grandpa. Knowing that was something nobody could take from her.

She sucked in a deep breath, feeling full and sweet on the inside and safe and strong on the outside, just like a Jelly Heart donut with its armor of sugary sprinkles!

"You're a rotten man," Mattie said, pointing at Ace. "And *you*"—Mattie faced Adelaide. "That gloopy oil could ruin the river. Why would you mess things up if you want to build a stupid hotel? People are *still* cleaning that ditch!"

"Who cares?" Adelaide said. "We'll pay the cleanup fines for your aunt, tear down that ridiculous donut shop, and put up a real money maker. It's just a little cooking oil, right, Uncle Ace?"

Ace nodded, but behind his wicked smile, Mattie could see his real feelings. Adelaide had basically called him a fool for owning a donut shop in the first place. He looked guilty, like he knew it was all wrong. The gloop and the trick and the being jealous of another family for a million years.

That's when Beanie popped up from her corner and made a mad dash for the office door, knocking piles of magazines over as she ran.

Ace looked more confused than ever. He jerked out

of his leather chair but stood frozen behind his desk.

Adelaide huffed with impatience at Ace and clicked across the room in her shiny heels like a football player ready to tackle Beanie. She dove for the girl with her shiny red fingernails glinting.

Seeing someone come for her little sister snapped Sasha out of her scaredness. She tumbled out of her chair and sacked the real estate lady right in the guts.

Ooof.

The look on Adelaide's face was great. So great! Except that now she was mad and no way could she hide it anymore.

Beanie wove in and out of stacks of newspapers and magazines and knocked one of the folding chairs over. Clang! She zagged right around Adelaide, who sprang forward and slipped, her high heels flying off her feet. Beanie pushed the tallest stack of newspapers toward Adelaide and made it out into the hall.

Ace finally came to life, his nose turning purple all over again as he lunged around the desk.

With the newspapers piled on top of her, Adelaide lay out on the floor like a dead starfish covered in seaweed. Mattie and Sasha hopped over her and followed Beanie out into the hall.

Beanie was racing away.

The *wrong* way.

To the front of the shop, where the door was sure to be locked.

"Beanieeeee!" both girls shouted.

They raced after her. The light of the sunset outside turned the front windows rosy orange. Adelaide and Ace tumbled down the hall right after them. Beanie tried to open the front door, pulling on the metal handle. Bang-bang bangity-bang bang.

Ace lurched toward Mattie and Sasha until the two of them were backed up against the shop's display case. Mattie watched breathlessly as Adelaide closed in on Beanie. The look on Beanie's face was all bug-eyed. More scared than if they were watching a scary part in a movie and she asked them to pause it. She was holding Mr. Little's phone in her hands and trying to call somebody, but her hands were shaking and the phone clattered to the floor.

Ace loomed closer, pushing Sasha and Mattie back behind the donut shop counter and farther and farther from Beanie. Mattie and Sasha looked at each other and both grabbed a handful of stray stale chocolate donuts, pelting Ace with them.

Thunk.

Thunk.

Thunk.

Mattie grabbed a heavy bag of powdered sugar next, heaving it at Ace. He caught the bag, but a giant poof of powdered sugar exploded all over him, turning him into something like one of Aunt Molly's Powdered Puffies. He rubbed at his eyes, coughing and sputtering in the sugary cloud. But Adelaide was still moving toward Beanie in her bare feet.

She picked up the newly cracked phone, furious, and slunk toward the fryer. She pushed past Sasha and Mattie, shot a frustrated look to her powdered-sugar-coated uncle, and held the phone up with a flourish.

Flump.

It dropped into the gloopy oil like a raw donut. And it was ruined. Forever. How would they call for help now?

Mattie pulled her arm back, aimed, and pelted Adelaide as hard as she could with the last stale donut.

She reached around for something else to throw.

But there was nothing left.

Adelaide grinned like a vampire.

Then Mattie saw a dark shadow flash across the front windows. Boom! Something flopped against the window. Something with two golden eyes.

Boom! It was Alfred, landing on the windowsill, smacking against the glass. He winked, wobbled, then took off again to swoop over the street. He dove near an oncoming car, and Mattie flinched when he came close, the car skidding to a stop with squealing brakes.

Alfred banked and dove past another car, a green one, swooping so close it swerved and bumped into a parked car. The dented car's horn began to honk in an endless loop. Beep. Beep. Beep. Alfred banked again and landed on the elegant curve of the streetlight.

Adelaide marched toward Mattie and Sasha. "Get the little one away from the window," she said to Ace. But before Ace could grab Beanie, Mattie heard something else. A siren.

Lights flashed against the display case of Ace's Excellent Donuts. Beanie stopped yanking on the locked door.

"It's the police!" she said, peering down the street on her tiptoes.

Ace and Adelaide both turned to watch the lights bouncing around the shop. Then they made a run for it.

Straight out into the stinky alley.

THE DOUBLE DECKER DONUT BOX
OUR SIGNATURE ASSORTMENT OF DONUTS IS PERFECT FOR ANY CELEBRATION. EACH BOX CONTAINS BANANA SLUG BARS, SQUIRREL SPECIALS, TURKEY TALONS, BIG SUR SUNSETS, AND AN ASSORTMENT OF SPECIAL SELECTIONS.

As the owl flies, the distance between Big Sur and Monterey is roughly thirty miles. Alfred's top speed, in his prime, topped out at forty miles per hour. Alfred was no longer in his prime. After a couple hours of stops and starts, he'd landed on a craggy bit of rock above a scenic turnout. Loads of tourists had pulled to the side, taking pictures of the Bixby Creek Bridge, which arched elegantly over the rocky shoreline.

Weighing several options, he eyed the back of a motor home slowly pulling onto the highway. There was not a moment to waste. He lifted his wings, banked, and landed with a thud, fixing his talons to the latch of the motor home sunroof. Alfred willed himself into stillness, hoping any travelers he passed would assume he was one of those horrible owls of the plastic variety, meant to frighten off all sorts of less intimidating creatures.

By the time he arrived in Monterey, his dignity, and some of his feathers, were in a state of disarray. But his eyes were as sharp as ever. When Mattie went in—but did not come out of—the donut shop, dignity became the least of Alfred's worries. He needed to make a spectacle of himself.

And he did so with flair.

His wild swooping brought forth from the center of the city a bright red fire engine, a black-and-white police car, and an animal control truck, which Alfred had no intention of getting into.

As soon as he spied the gloopers in the alleyway behind the shop, he left his perch atop the streetlight, took a wild dive past the police officer exiting his vehicle, and flew on soundless wings for the back alley. A disgruntled man in blue and two tan-uniformed animal control officers scrambled right behind him.

Turning the corner and flapping for the sky, Alfred watched with relish as Ace and Adelaide ran smack into the first officer on scene. A very satisfying poof of powdered sugar followed.

The startled police officer had things well in hand as Alfred disappeared into the gloom of evening. "What's the rush?" the officer said, pulling a flashlight from his belt. "Would you two stand against the wall, please?"

Mattie was the first of the girls to poke her nose out into the alley. Ace and Adelaide were pressed up against the alley wall with a light shining in their eyes. Adelaide was flashing her perfect smile and telling a wild story. All about how crazy this kid was and how she was upset about losing her family business. Blah, blah, blah! Mattie could also tell that the officer wasn't buying it for a second.

"These two," Mattie said, "basically kidnapped us."

Sasha bugged her eyes out, like *maybe* that was stretching the truth, but Beanie backed Mattie up right away. She pointed at Adelaide. "That one stole my dad's phone right out of my hand and plopped it into some kitchen gloop."

The whole story took a while to tell, and for a few minutes, Mattie wasn't sure who the police officers were going to believe. It sure didn't help that the animal control people were shining their lights around the whole time, looking for a crazed owl.

But then the man from the photography shop turned up.

As it turned out, he'd recognized the logo in that picture too. He'd been more than a little suspicious and had made double prints of all the photos from Sasha's camera. Otto—that was his actual name—arrived in the middle of all Adelaide's arguing, alarmed after hearing sirens near the donut shop up the street so soon after he'd found its logo in the girls' strange photos. He told the officers that his husband had *insisted* the photos be turned over to the police, which Otto had assumed was a silly idea until he'd heard those sirens. He raised his bushy eyebrows when he said the word *sirens*, and it made Mattie smile.

Otto smiled back.

That's when the officers finally got around to putting Ace and Adelaide into handcuffs. Afterward, they asked the girls to explain everything once more from the beginning. Sasha had a lot of trouble telling a straight story. She was so mad that she kept leaving things out. But Mattie took a deep breath and started with the tapping at her window, telling everything to an officer in a midnight blue uniform. Her badge glinted like the stars.

Soon Deputy Nuñez showed up, and Mattie was all-the-way glad to see him. He talked to the city police officers and filled them in on what had been going on in Big Sur. His brown uniform and their blue ones looked like the sand and the sky to Mattie. Everything would be all right now. Deputy Nuñez even apologized to Mattie about not taking her seriously, which was something Mattie didn't think he did very often. Or ever. Then he drove the girls back home. They played Jell-O in the back seat.

"Mattie," Deputy Nuñez said, about halfway to Big Sur. "Those pictures you girls got, and your statements . . . They might be enough to send those crooks to jail. But they might not."

Beanie stopped playing Jell-O and sat straight up in her seat, straining against her seatbelt. "Well, *I* got their confession on Dad's phone. That's always enough in the movies."

"Beanie," Sasha sighed, "you watch too many movies. Besides, Dad's phone is at the bottom of a vat of oil."

"Dad's *phone* is, but those stinkers' confessions aren't. I sent it to Mom right before I made a run for it. It *is* in slow motion, though. I think. I can never figure that button out."

"Beanieeee!" both girls said.

"What?" she asked.

And neither of them had anything to say whatsoever. They leaned in and hugged her. They didn't play any more Jell-O after that, because Beanie fell asleep. Deputy Nuñez dropped the girls off soon after that, and they got wrapped in blankets and tucked into bed.

The next morning, Mattie learned that the news about the real gloopers had traveled quickly. Even on a holiday weekend. Aunt Molly threw the contract to sell Owl's straight into the recycling. She'd never signed it. The yellow hazard tape was still up across the highway, but the angry red signs from the health department and the Environmental Services Agency had been taken off of Owl's front door. The agency had dropped its enforcement case against Aunt Molly too. It had a new rotten fish to fry.

Besides, the well water had been tested, and it was fine for making donuts, and did Aunt Molly ever make donuts. She must have stayed up all night, right through Monday morning. When Mattie woke up, the trailer was empty, and she could see Martín and Aunt Molly buzzing around the shop with trays and trays and trays of treats.

The display case was a rainbow of sprinkles all over again. There was a line at Owl's from 6 a.m. until closing. It seemed like every single person in Big Sur needed a huge box of donuts that day. They ordered double decker deluxe boxes for parties and picnics and meetings and for no reason at all.

Even Hermit Harriet came and ordered a double decker box. Which was the weirdest thing to ever happen in the history of Owl's Outstanding Donuts, because all she'd ever ordered before was a single cup of black coffee.

Mattie wondered what Harriet was really going to do with all those donuts.

Eat them?

All by herself?

The only person who didn't order a single thing was Mrs. Mantooth, who stood at the end of her driveway to keep customers from backing up the wrong way. She yelled at four different people before she gave up and went home. But at least she didn't pester Aunt Molly about buying a new pump for their well. Not that day, anyway.

Mr. and Mrs. Little ordered ten double decker boxes for the big Labor Day weekend pool party at the campground. Those ten boxes had to be delivered. In a car. Mattie rode over in the passenger's seat.

Her pink sparkly swimsuit itched at her from under her clothes as she carried the boxes down to the party.

Kids were already splashing in the pool, and the sun shone through the redwoods and lit up the big fluffy sycamore leaves like party lanterns.

"Beanie, no offense, but this is going to be way more fun than your birthday," Mattie said, grinning.

Beanie didn't take offense, but she did push Mattie into the pool.

They played Marco Polo with all the kids from school, and everybody knew that Aunt Molly's donut shop was saved and that Mattie wasn't going to have to move and that the Waters weren't the gloopers and that those grumps were going to jail, all because of Beanie's slow-motion evidence.

There was a diving contest, which Beanie declared she won by doing a cannon ball with a yodel attached.

"Yodelodelodelooooooo!"

Mattie didn't mind not winning, but Sasha crossed her arms. Then Christian did a perfect dive and bopped Beanie on the head with a pool noodle over and over until she admitted defeat. He did a victory underwater summersault next. When he popped out of the water, his smile was shiny like sun sparkling on a wave. It made

Mattie feel fizzy inside. Okay, so she didn't exactly hate Christian Castillo.

Sasha smirked at Mattie, like she could tell just what Mattie was thinking. As that little secret passed between them, some of the weirdness of all of them being together evaporated like water on the pool deck.

Halfway through the party, after veggie burgers and hot dogs and potato salad and chips and salsa, a flock of wild turkeys went strutting by. One of the turkeys had an entire Big Sur Sunset donut in its beak, and the whole flock was chasing it, gobbling and pecking each other down to the river. Aunt Molly whispered in Mattie's ear, and Mattie smiled. It turned out Harriet Hargrave and Grandpa Herman had been carpentry buddies, and Harriet couldn't resist helping Owl's out by buying all those donuts, even if she was only going to give them to the wild turkeys.

Seeing the turkeys made Mattie worry, just a little, about Alfred and those animal control officers. He couldn't have gotten caught, could he? All day, Mattie peeked around the trees, searching for two golden polka dots or signs of shivery owl feathers. She didn't see them. She didn't see Alfred.

But she believed, absolutely, that she would.

THE OLD FASHIONED OWL
A SIMPLE CAKE DONUT WITH A DASH OF SOMETHING SECRET

That Monday night, the last night of summer, Mattie helped Aunt Molly clean empty donut trays and load them into the gleaming donut case. They had officially sold out.

"So . . . there's no sign of your owl friend, huh?" Aunt Molly asked.

"Nope," Mattie shook her head.

Molly reached into the donut case and clicked the display light off. Then she thunked a Strawberry Iced Classic into the palm of Mattie's hand. "Well, just in case things turn around, why don't you leave this out? You said they're his favorite, so I saved one."

Mattie couldn't tell how much Aunt Molly really believed about that owl and how much she thought Mattie made up. The donut in her hand was not so much proof of Aunt Molly's believing but of her love.

Aunt Molly smiled and turned around on her squeaky sneakers to arrange stacks of empty pink boxes with little slips of paper taped to them. They'd sit on the back counter until the next morning, when Molly would have twenty more double decker donut box orders to fill.

Aunt Molly double-checked each order form, not slowing down for a second, not looking suspicious.

"I'll be home after we close up," Aunt Molly said. "Go get to bed. You've got a big day tomorrow."

Martín swished past Mattie with the mop.

"G'night Martín," Mattie said.

He spun the mop around, swishing it all around her until she giggled. "Feliz noche, Mattie," he said. And he was right, it was a great night.

Mattie walked home alone. The wind pricked up the hair along her arms. The crickets hummed, and a very serious toad was serenading the sky from somewhere down in the river. The redwoods soared upward like dark towers, but there was still no sign of Alfred.

Mattie turned back to check the shop. The outlines of Martín and Aunt Molly at closing time were like dancers who did the same routine every night. Mop the floors, shine the case, take out the trash. Even though they were indoors, it was like they could hear the music of crickets and toads and pounding Big Sur waves. Mattie turned and walked home, feeling like her steps matched that music too.

In the trailer, Mattie had everything lined up for the next day. She had a rainbow of pencils with perfect pink eraser tops. She had three highlighters, four notebooks, a calculator, a protractor, and a florescent pink ruler all packed neatly into her sparkling turquoise backpack. Aunt Molly would slip her favorite lunch into it in the morning. A pesto, cucumber, and cheese sandwich, potato chips, guava juice, and her favorite donut: The Old Fashioned Owl.

Mattie hadn't really ever thought about how that donut got its name before. Aunt Molly insisted that Mattie's mom had named it and that Grandma and Grandpa liked the idea since it matched that old sign they'd found. Mattie loved knowing the secret ingredient. A dash of nutmeg.

She slipped on a fresh pair of pajama pants and the soft old T-shirt that had been her mom's. Then she snuck out onto the deck, balanced the pink donut on the rail, and listened.

But Alfred's swoop was silent.

Mostly.

He landed on the rail and hopped several times to catch his balance. Crump-crump-crump. Mattie giggled. Alfred bent toward the donut and clacked his beak with pleasure.

"I thought about bringing you a Slug Bar," Mattie said with a crooked smile. Alfred rustled his feathers, mildly offended. "Aunt Molly made a bunch for the double decker boxes. But those are mostly for tourists, and we're both home."

Alfred leaned closer and twitched his ear tufts upward.

Saying the word *home* made a shiver race down Mattie's back.

"Did you come to wish me good luck for my first day of school tomorrow?" Mattie asked.

Alfred blinked yes.

That's what it felt like, anyway, and sometimes the way something feels is the way it is. The glittery gold of Alfred's eyes reminded Mattie of the school bus, but she wasn't afraid of that anymore. With the donut shop saved and Sasha back in her best-friend corner, Mattie knew she was ready to ride up Highway One for fifth grade with Sasha . . . and Christian. Beanie was going to ride with them too, but she was only a second grader, which Sasha said barely counts.

There were only two questions Mattie had left to ask Alfred. Questions she didn't even know she wanted to ask before. Mattie edged closer to Alfred, and he rustled his feathers.

She'd decided to keep going. To grow up and go to fifth grade, because Mom wouldn't have wanted her be afraid of moving forward. But if she kept growing up, would Alfred still be her friend? She didn't know any grown-ups who talked to owls. It was something that was starting to worry her.

Mattie took a deep breath.

"Will you . . . will you ever stop talking to me, Alfred?"

Alfred swiveled his head away, to watch the sliver of

ocean shushing below the cliffs. The stars twinkled, and a car swooshed around the bend and didn't stop. When he looked back, Mattie stared at him until he pressed his ear tufts down and clacked his beak.

Of course not.

Mattie smiled. "I'd never stop talking to you either, Alfred. I promise."

Alfred edged toward the pink donut.

"Just one more question," Mattie said. "Do you think I'll ever stop missing her?"

This time Alfred did not look away. He clacked his beak and hopped so close to Mattie that his feathers brushed her arm.

Mattie blinked at the stars and wiped at her face.

They stood there together, just enjoying the night, listening to the cars whoosh by on the highway. Side by side, standing watch over their home. Mattie was glad to be where she was. With Alfred and Aunt Molly and Sasha and Beanie. She didn't feel bad loving Big Sur so much anymore. She could love it and miss her mom too. At the same time.

Finally, the sign for Owl's Outstanding Donuts, which stood watch over them all, flickered off for the night.

"Goodnight, Alfred," Mattie said, backing toward the trailer before Aunt Molly could come clanging out the back door of the donut shop.

Alfred hooted deeply, clutched the pink donut, and

swooped across the parking lot. He beat his wings, banked, and flew over the highway. Against the inky sky, the pink treat in his talons was like a shooting star from a dream. His hoots echoed through the trees and past the highway and out over the ocean. Who-who-whooooo . . .

That night, Alfred knew that Mattie would fall asleep with the sounds of Big Sur echoing in her heart, a sound that Alfred could hear nearly a mile away. Maybe farther. A sound that Alfred knew he would never stop listening for, whether Mattie remembered her promise or not. But Alfred believed with every feather that she would.

THE DELUXE DOUBLE DECKER DONUT BOX

Special Order Form

Select up to 24 donuts to build a box full of dreams!

The Strawberry Iced Classic: ___   The Sprinkle Emergency: ___

The Banana Slug Bar: ___   The S'more Bomb: ___

The Chocolate Rainbow: ___   The Birthday Bar: ___

The Turkey Talon: ___   The Boysenberry Beauty: ___

The Golden Galaxy: ___   The Velvet Vampire: ___

The Donut Hole (1 dozen): ___   The Vegan Maple Bacon Bar: ___

The Banana Boat: ___   The Campfire Cruller: ___

The Jelly Heart: ___   The Chocolate Twist: ___

The Squirrel Special: ___   The Cardamom Classic: ___

The Blue Moon: ___   The Tart Turnover: ___

The Big Sur Sunset: ___   The Powdered Puffies: ___

The Old Fashioned Owl: ___

ACKNOWLEDGMENTS

This book began with an image stolen (with permission) from the mind of Teagan White, and so she is due the first word of thanks. I may be a thief, but like Alfred, I have my integrity. Teagan dreamt of an owl purloining pink-frosted donuts in the night, and it was an idea I found irresistible. Thanks for letting me sneak it onto my plate.

This book was baked with the help of many hands, each adding their own secret ingredient. Thank you to Kelsey King for such an outstanding and colorful cover. Thank you to my former agent Caryn Wiseman, who shepherded this project from proposal to acceptance. And thank you to everyone at Lerner from acquisitions to customer service (where the most perfectly packed boxes of books are baked). Thank you to Libby Stille and Lindsay Matvick for spreading the word about Alfred and Mattie—hoot-hoot! You all have my sincerest gratitude for getting *Owl's* into the hands of teachers, librarians, and young readers.

Special appreciation must be given to Emily Harris, who is able to turn my hopeful design notes into impeccable realities and always leaves a shiny surprise under the dust jacket for her authors. A deluxe box of donuts should go to Greg Hunter as a prize for his faith, patience, nudging, and nurturing of this book into existence. And a decadent-dark-chocolate-glazed thank you goes to all of my writing friends and critique partners.

Last, thank you to Big Sur and its beauty. To banana slugs and tall trees and all the people who work to keep places wild and healthy, green and blue, and free of gloop!

ABOUT THE AUTHOR

Robin Yardi lives in the California foothills, where—every once in a while, in the dark of night—a great horned owl will hoot. She loves good stories, animals of all sorts, homemade cakes, and kids. She thinks kids are way cooler than grownups, which is why she writes just for them. Visit her online at www.robinyardi.com.